JINGLE ALL THE WAY

A SADDLE HILL CHRISTMAS MYSTERY

ERIN LANTER

ISBN: 978-1-7357188-8-0
ISBN (e-book): 978-1-7357188-9-7

Also by Erin Lanter:

The Dark Hour

Buried Secrets

Saddle Hill Christmas Mysteries:

Follow That Star

I'll Be Home for Christmas

Jingle All the Way

For Barbara Napier and Snug Hollow Farm Bed & Breakfast.
Thank you for sharing your slice of paradise.

JINGLE ALL THE WAY

Chapter One

SLEET TAPPED AGAINST the window over the kitchen sink as Marian Bright pulled the roasting pan out of the oven and wiped her hands on her apron. The kitchen smelled of roast chicken and rosemary—just the thing to bring a feeling of warmth and comfort to a blustery mid-December evening. Complete with sautéed green beans, garlic-and-Parmesan mashed potatoes, and homemade sourdough rolls, it was a meal that would warm her guests from the inside out.

"It looks like we're going to have a full house again tonight," Nadine Adler said as she pushed open the swinging door that connected the dining room to the kitchen.

A grin spread across Marian's face. "Business has been good since we opened, but I never could have imagined it would be as good as it has been the last few weeks."

When Marian decided to buy this old farmhouse after she'd been held captive in it by a kidnapper last year, her only goal had been to return it to its former use as a bed-and-breakfast. After many months of renovation and repair, it was a place that felt like home not only to her, but to her guests as well. Marian made sure of that by placing a small basket of baked goods and a variety of hot teas, hot chocolate, and coffee in each room for the guests.

"Any new folks tonight?" Marian asked Nadine. She'd been so busy in the kitchen that she hadn't even had time to look at the reservation list.

Nadine's head bobbed up and down. "A few. We have a recently retired professor here with his wife—the Hubleys. They're obviously from out of town and have the garden-view room." Nadine lowered her voice and leaned toward Marian. "They seem a bit dull, if you ask me. A young couple that doesn't talk much to anyone but each other is in the big suite upstairs. There's something about them that bugs me. They certainly don't look like they'd be able to afford that room. We've also got a middle-aged woman in the smallest room who is here solo. My guess is she's a cat lady. I wouldn't be surprised if she smuggled one in in that big purse of hers." A small giggle escaped Nadine's throat.

Marian's mouth drooped at one corner. "I certainly hope not. After all the work we've put in to this place, I don't want it to smell like cat pee. And I hope the professor doesn't expect much of a view. By this time of year, the garden is long gone."

"Anybody with half a brain would know there isn't much growing in December." With a wink, Nadine added, "A retired professor should have at least that much."

A chuckle rose up in Marian's throat, and she reminded herself again how fortunate she was that Nadine had agreed to leave the Rose Petal Café and work full-time for her at the bed-and-breakfast. Though owning her own restaurant had been

Nadine's dream, things changed with the arrival of her baby girl in the spring. Nadine's husband, Joe, was sheriff of Saddle Hill and always seemed to be called out for one thing or another. A job with fewer responsibilities and more flexibility and where her baby was welcome was just what Nadine needed now that she was a mother.

"How many others will be joining us for dinner?" Marian queried.

Nadine shrugged. "The usual crew. Sylvia, Ralph and Carla, Kris, James and Patricia. I think Holly and Eli are also going to try to make it. Probably about thirteen total."

"Other than Kris, everyone else is perfectly capable of making their own dinner," Marian said. "I don't know why they'd want to come all the way out here and spend this kind of money on a dinner when they could just as easily eat at home. Our location isn't exactly convenient."

Taking a few steps forward, Nadine came around beside Marian and slipped her arm around the older woman's shoulders. "I think they come because they love you and want to support you. It might be easier for them to eat at home than drive all the way out here, but where's the fun in that, especially around the holidays? Ask any of them, and they'll tell you they want to be with family for Christmas, and we're all family."

Warmth crept up Marian's spine. She was blessed with a terrific group of friends. Even though they were all different ages and came from all walks of life, their friendship worked somehow. Because of the trouble they'd all faced the past couple Christmases, they'd forged a bond that was deeper than friendship. Marian, widowed at age seventy-one, would never be alone again. Not if this group had anything to say about it.

Chapter Two

SYLVIA BELL BUTTONED her coat and slipped her feet into her fur-lined winter boots. Dinner at the Farmhouse Inn would be served in an hour. If she left now, after a thirty-minute drive to the outskirts of town, she'd still have about a half hour to visit with the other regulars and maybe get to know some of the new faces that were calling the bed-and-breakfast home for the next day or two.

As she wrapped a scarf around her neck, Sylvia inhaled the scent of cedar and lavender that had become the signature scent of her Saddle Hill home, and loathed the fact that she couldn't spend more time here. The modern farmhouse decor she'd chosen felt like a big hug every time she walked through the door. It was cozy in a way she never thought she'd be able to appreciate. Here, she wasn't concerned with the clean lines and matching pieces of furniture that dominated her Park Avenue apartment. In this house, every piece she purchased was selected not because of how it looked, but because of how it made her *feel*, how easy it was to sink into it and forget about the stress of her everyday life.

Being a fashion designer had been a dream of hers for as long as she could remember. Now in her early forties, though, she'd begun to wonder if maybe it was time to slow down. The thought of stepping away from the fashion empire she'd spent the better part of fifteen years building made her nearly break out in a nervous sweat. It was all she knew. Besides, what would she do with her time if she weren't running the company? And what would happen to all the people who worked for her? She supposed she could just step aside and let the second-in-command take over the day-to-day responsibilities while she maintained creative control over the actual designs, but would that actually work, or was it just wishful thinking? Sylvia shook her head firmly. This wasn't the time to make life-altering decisions. The stress of the holidays didn't need to launch a full-blown mid-life crisis.

Determined to enjoy the next ten days at her home away from home, she squelched the thoughts that had become more and more frequent and checked herself in the mirror that hung above the overstuffed cream-colored sofa. Her dark hair showed no trace of gray, and the only wrinkles on her face were faint smile lines around her eyes. The sign of a happy life, she'd reminded herself more than once when she wondered if age was going to start taking its toll. She didn't look like she was in her forties, she assured herself, and she knew she still turned heads. Until now, though, she hadn't been all that concerned with her love life.

"Which is probably why I don't have one," she muttered under her breath.

There just wasn't time. Any of the halfway decent guys she met were interested in settling down at some point. With her career and the long hours she put in, settling down was something she just couldn't commit to. With each passing holiday, though, she was painfully aware that the clock was ticking. There were few unattached men her age, and from her experience, most of them were unattached for a reason.

Shaking her head again, Sylvia commanded through clenched teeth, "Get a hold of yourself. Stop thinking like this and go enjoy dinner with your friends."

This was the most wonderful time of the year, after all, and Saddle Hill was the most comforting place on earth. The bed-and-breakfast would be decorated for Christmas and Marian would have gone all out in creating a welcoming and cozy atmosphere. She hadn't been there yet during the Christmas season, and she couldn't wait to see what Marian and Nadine had done with the place. She'd also heard that Marian hired a new girl—Marie or Michelle or something that started with an "M," she thought but wasn't sure—to help with setting up and serving dinner. Sylvia couldn't wait to meet her.

With a renewed bounce in her step, Sylvia grabbed her purse from the hook and went into the garage. As she backed out and sleet pinged against the hood of her car, she was thankful she'd invested in having the garage added to the house. It would have taken forever to scrape this ice off her windshield.

Skidding slightly at the end of the driveway, Sylvia reminded herself she'd need to be careful. Memories of the treacherous road conditions last Christmas when she'd driven out to the farmhouse with the sheriff and deputy to look for Marian flashed in her mind. They'd even been in an accident due to the slippery roads.

Maybe I should stay home tonight, Sylvia considered. The roads could be dangerous.

Against her better judgment, she kept her car pointed in the direction of Broken Branch Road and the Farmhouse Inn Bed & Breakfast. Confident that she'd become a proficient driver on Saddle Hill's rural roads over the past couple of years, she pressed onward, careful not to go too fast. The accident last winter had sufficiently shaken her up, and she didn't want a repeat of that experience.

Tonight would be the night she officially kicked off her vacation and the holiday season in Saddle Hill. There was no way she was going to let anything spoil it.

Chapter Three

"ARE YOU ALMOST ready?" Eli Nolan called to Holly, his wife of two months.

"Coming!" she shouted from their bedroom.

Eli's fingers, which had been drumming the coffee table for the last minute or so, stilled when Holly emerged from the hall leading from the bedroom to the living room.

"Wow," he said, shaking his head. "Just when I think I get used to how pretty you are, you surprise me again."

Pink crept up Holly's neck and found its way to her cheeks. "Thanks," she muttered, tucking her hair behind her ear. It was a nervous habit she'd picked up, and Eli thought it was adorable.

"Ready?" he asked, then raised himself from his perched position on the edge of the sofa.

"Two minutes," Holly replied, then walked to the kitchen and took a wrapped package from the top of the refrigerator.

"What's that?"

"A Christmas present for Marian. She's been so good to me the last few years. It won't come close to thanking her, but at least it's something," Holly said with a shrug.

Eli walked up behind Holly and slid his arms around his bride's waist. "She's been good to both of us. I still can't believe she actually *gave* us this house as a wedding present."

Holly nodded in agreement. They had both been stunned when, as a wedding present, Marian had deeded the house to them. Since opening the bed-and-breakfast, Marian thought it would be best if she stayed on the property. After several months of work, the renovation of the old barn that sat a few hundred yards from the farmhouse was finally complete. What was once a drafty old dump-heap was now a charming dwelling that Marian treasured. It was just like Marian to turn something that should have held nothing but bad memories into a beautiful place that would allow good memories to be made for years to come.

Tears welled in Holly's eyes. "She said she always knew she'd have to leave this house at some point, but that it was easier now that she had family to give it to." She sniffled. "I've never had family like that."

"Now you do," Eli said as he turned Holly around to study her features, his eyes landing on her straight nose with a spray of freckles across it. "I know you had a tough time growing up, with your parents getting divorced around Christmas and then their hostility toward each other, but you can be sure that the rest of your life is going to look a lot different."

Holly inhaled and looked around the kitchen, then into the living room. Very little had changed about the house since she came to live here two Christmases ago. Marian had even left all the furniture.

Except Roger's favorite chair. That was one thing Marian would never part with. She insisted it still held traces of Roger's aftershave, though Holly had never been able to smell anything.

All because Marian had taken an interest in a troubled young woman who needed a fresh start, Holly now had a home—and a family. A smile tugged at Holly's lips. So many good memories have been made here in such a short amount of time. She hadn't been able to bring herself to move into Marian's room, which was larger than her own and had an attached bathroom. Instead, she and Eli slept in the room she moved into when Marian took her in. The pine furniture and flannel bedding was just as cozy as it always had been. Maybe even more so now that she had someone to share it with.

"Remembering?" Eli asked, just as he did every time Holly got that wistful, faraway look in her eyes.

Holly nodded. "I am," she agreed. "I owe everything to Marian. Because of her, I have a family. A real family that cares about and looks out for each other." She turned her gaze to Eli's adoring eyes. "Not to mention that if she hadn't taken me in, I never would have met you."

"Glad I at least got an honorable mention," he teased. "But if we want to be on time for dinner, we've got to leave now," he reminded her.

"I'm ready," she said, hugging the wrapped package to her chest.

They walked to the car, sleet already beginning to fall even though it hadn't been predicted until later.

"Should we stay home?" Holly worried aloud, her voice communicating how disappointed she'd be if they missed this dinner.

"It'll be fine," Eli assured her as he opened the car door for her. "I've driven on the roads out there in worse conditions than this."

Holly slid into the passenger-side seat and grabbed the seat-belt, ready to buckle it. "Yeah, but you were in a wreck on the way out there last year when the roads were in bad condition," she reminded him.

"And I learned something from it," he said, then shut the door and circled the car to slide behind the steering wheel.

"What's that?"

"I learned not to wreck again," Eli said with a wink.

"I hope so," Holly muttered worriedly, then leaned her head back against the seat, saying a silent prayer that they'd be safe and that nothing would go wrong this Christmas.

Chapter Four

VITO FRANKS PUSHED the door leading from the mudroom to the kitchen open with his foot. His arms loaded with firewood, he gave a slight nod to Marian and Nadine as he made his way into the living room. Marian had specifically requested a roaring fire to set the tone for the evening, especially since they had some first-time guests staying at the bed-and-breakfast.

Taking one log at a time from his left arm, he gently placed them in the log holder to the right of the fireplace. After the last log was in the holder, Vito glanced above the mantle and smiled. There, looking back at him, was a clock made from an old tiller blade and white chalk paint.

This time last year had been so different. Last Christmas he'd been down on his luck, and in an act of desperation, took on the job of kidnapping Marian. He'd never met the person that offered him twenty-five thousand dollars to hold her captive in this house, but when bills were looming and his stomach was hungry, it seemed like a good idea.

He shook his head, a sliver of shame trying to worm its way back into his mind. Marian had forgiven him and made sure he didn't have to spend any time in jail. More than that, she'd offered him a job and a home.

For the better part of the last year, Vito had spent his days working on the dilapidated farmhouse and turning it into a dream getaway location for those valuing a slower-paced vacation. Now as he looked around the living room at the high ceilings and the fresh paint, he was reminded again how much a little TLC can change a place—or person.

After all, he was living proof.

"Is it all coming back to you?" said a gentle voice from behind Vito.

He turned and looked into the face of his kidnapping-victim-turned-friend. Marian was smiling as only she could, reminding him of the goodness in the world.

Vito nodded gently. "I am. This place turned out really incredible, if I do say so myself."

"Well, if you don't say it, I will," Marian teased. "You did a first-rate job fixing this place up. Not to mention the barn. I never thought I would be living in a barn."

"It only looks like a barn from the outside," Vito countered. "On the inside, it bears no resemblance to a place that once housed farm animals and rusty old tools."

"No, it certainly doesn't," Marian agreed, "and that's to your credit." She glanced at the clock above the mantle. "We'll be serving dinner in about a half hour. Can you get this fire blazing before they get here?"

"How many are you expecting tonight?"

"Somewhere between twelve and fifteen, counting local friends and the guests who are staying here."

Vito chewed his bottom lip and looked at the toes of his work boots. "Will Sylvia be here?"

Marian grinned. "As a matter of fact, she will. Why do you ask?"

Vito lifted his eyes to meet Marian's. "I, uh, it's just that, uh…" he stammered.

Marian's grin turned into laughter. "It's just that you've been sweet on her since the day she showed up here with Holly and Nadine looking for me. Am I right?"

With his face a shade of crimson that was somewhere between angry and embarrassed, he mumbled, "I was just wondering."

Patting his shoulder before turning to go back to the kitchen, Marian said, "She'll be here soon, and with as cold as it is outside, I'm sure you'll want her to have a nice fire to cozy up next to." With that, Marian disappeared into the kitchen to supervise the final touches of this evening's dinner.

Vito exhaled sharply. Marian was right. He'd fallen for Sylvia the first time he'd laid eyes on her. Things would never work out, though, he'd reminded himself hundreds of times during the past year. They couldn't be more different. Besides, she didn't even live around here, and her occasional visits to Saddle Hill weren't enough to make any kind of relationship work. Not to mention the fact that he was in no way cut out for life in New York.

He was blue-collar and she was Park Avenue.

Even so, he couldn't deny that his heart beat a little faster any time she was around. He shook the thought away and stacked some logs in the fireplace. As he struck a match and watched the flames grow, he decided that even if he couldn't ever be part of her life the way he wanted to be, he could at least make sure she had a warm place to be after she came in from the cold.

Chapter Five

"HOW DO I look?" Louise Hubley asked her husband as she smoothed the pleats of her tweed skirt with her palms.

"Like the wife of a recently retired college professor," her husband said from his chair by the fireplace with a twinkle in his eye.

"Oh, Grant. Does that mean I look boring?" Louise worried aloud.

Grant Hubley raised his lanky body from the chair he'd been sitting in. "Not to worry, dear. You look wonderful. It's just that I'm looking forward to this next chapter of my life—of our lives, and believe me when I tell you there won't be anything boring about it."

Louise unconsciously patted her graying hair, twisted into a loose bun. "I know you're excited, but it might take a little time to get used to my new role. My life is affected by your choices, too."

Grant looked at his wife affectionately and pulled her into

a tight hug. "You have always been so supportive of me and my ambitions. I can't tell you how much I appreciate having you by my side in all my endeavors." He planted a quick kiss on her cheek, then released her.

Taking a quick glance at herself in the full-length mirror that hung on the wall next to the bed, Louise once again smoothed the front of her skirt, straightened the buttons going down the front of her crisp, white shirt, and again patted her hair.

"Don't be nervous. They'll love you. People always love you," Grant assured his wife.

"I hope so," she murmured as she turned and peered over her shoulder, taking in her appearance from a different angle. "I always get so nervous every time we meet new people. What will they think of me? What if they don't like me? What if they think I can't be trusted?"

A small smile tugged at the corner of Grant's mouth. Only he knew the places where her confidence was lacking. "They'll think you're brilliant, charming, and beautiful, because that's what you are."

Heat crept up Louise's neck and settled in her cheeks. "You're just saying that."

"I'm saying that because it's true," Grant promised her. He tugged on his vest and straightened his back. "Ready for dinner?"

Louise nodded and glanced around their suite. It certainly was beautiful, and she was sure that the view was breathtaking in the springtime when the flowers and trees came to life. Even so, this place was so unlike anywhere they'd ever gone. "I don't know how I let you talk me into coming to a bed-and-breakfast in the middle of nowhere. From what I can tell, there is nothing to do. And it's on a farm. We're hardly farm folks."

"Just exploring options for the next part of our lives," Grant said with a wink, then turned and placed a hand on the doorknob of their suite. "Besides, this place has gotten great reviews and so many people have mentioned how amazing the food is. Try to loosen up and enjoy our mini vacation. You might have the time of your life."

Louise forced a smile and gave a slight nod of her head. Maybe this was a vacation for him, but despite his insistence that everything would be just fine, she was sure that trying to get everyone here to like her would be some of the hardest work she'd ever done.

Chapter Six

NADINE SET THE table with the personalized dinnerware Sylvia had given to Marian at the grand-opening celebration of the Farmhouse Inn. Thanks to Sylvia's friend who made custom pottery, the bed-and-breakfast now owned dishes that bore its name in a custom color now dubbed "Farmhouse White." Running her finger along the edge of the dinner plate in her hands, Nadine was able to feel the way each letter dipped into the smooth surface.

Carefully placing the plates on the red place mats, Nadine was again blown away by how the last year had gone. After pulling together every penny she and Joe had, she'd purchased the Rose Petal Café, where she'd worked as a pastry chef for many years. Even when she was pregnant with their daughter, Josephine, she'd continued to work the long hours necessary to keep a business running. The exhaustion worsened when the baby was born, and she found that the constant fatigue coupled with the gut-wrenching task of finding a nanny for their newborn was more than her heart could take. Nadine made the decision to sell the cafe and agreed to work for Marian—the only condition being that she could bring Josephine to work with her.

A smile lifted the corners of Nadine's mouth. It had been a good year.

"You've done a beautiful job with the table," Marian said from behind her.

Nadine's smile broadened. "It looks festive, doesn't it?"

The two women placed their hands on their hips as they studied the long table in front of them. Place settings for fifteen, the white plates against the red place mats were reminiscent of candy canes while the silverware glistened on each side. Fresh greens were arranged down the center of the table, with pine cones and poinsettia blooms scattered throughout. Flameless votive-sized candles in frosted-glass holders added a welcoming glow.

"Good call not using real candles for this arrangement," Marian commented. "It would be a real shame to see all the hard work we've put into this place go up in smoke if the greens caught on fire."

Nadine nodded in agreement, glad that Marian was pleased with the decor. Though she'd become quite good at decorating cookies, cakes, and other pastries in her time as a professional pastry chef, the thought of decorating anything else intimidated her. As far as she was concerned, her creativity began and ended in the kitchen.

"It looks really lovely, Nadine," Marian said warmly as she placed a hand on her younger friend's shoulder. "I don't know of anyone that could have done better."

"Thank you." Nadine dropped her gaze. "And thank you for this job. You don't know how much it means to me to be able to have Josephine with me at work. I'd thought owning the Rose Petal was my dream come true, but it's this. Working here with you is my dream come true."

Marian wrapped a slender arm around the middle of Nadine's back. "Dreams change, dear. I never thought I'd be doing this," she said, waving a hand around the room. "I'd never even considered opening a bed-and-breakfast, yet here I am, and I love every second of it."

Nadine chuckled. "I guess you never thought you'd be kidnapped and then fall in love with the house they kept you in."

Marian joined her laughter. "Not in a million years. I also didn't think I'd ever move out of the house where I lived with Roger to live in a barn, but life has a way of surprising us."

"I guess so."

"We've only got a half hour until dinner. Would you mind giving me a hand in the kitchen?" Marian asked.

"Sure thing. Mind if I check on Josie really quick first?" Nadine asked.

"No problem. Just come to the kitchen when you're finished," Marian agreed, then went through the swinging door that led to the kitchen.

Ten minutes later, Nadine and Marian worked side by side as they put the finishing touches on dinner. Soon the roast chicken, sautéed green beans, and potatoes were resting in their serving dishes, ready to be feasted upon by the guests at the inn.

When Marian ducked out of the kitchen for a few minutes, Nadine's eyes scanned the food. It looked—and smelled—delicious. At the sound of the kitchen door opening, Nadine turned slightly to see her husband, Sheriff Joe Adler, standing in the doorway.

"Joe!" Nadine exclaimed. "What are you doing here? I thought you were working tonight."

"I am, but I thought I'd drop by and see if you'd take pity on a poor, starving man's soul," Joe remarked with a twinkle in his eye. When she worked at the Rose Petal Café, he'd stop by frequently, asking the same question.

"Of course, but we have to make sure the paying guests get their food first," Nadine warned. "You can have the scraps."

"Is that any way to treat someone you've vowed to spend the rest of your life with?" he teased.

Nadine wrinkled her nose at him. "I'll do the best I can. This isn't my place. Marian has to give the okay for any food we give away."

"She already did. I called in advance." Joe stepped toward her and dropped a kiss on her cheek. "How's Josie?"

"Fine. I checked on her just a little while ago. She's sleeping."

"She does that a lot, doesn't she?" Joe observed.

Nadine nodded in agreement. "She's busy growing. She needs a lot of sleep."

At the sound of voices coming from the sitting room, Joe raised his eyebrows and said, "Sounds like the guests have arrived. The *paying* ones, anyway."

Giving his arm a playful swat, Nadine and Joe walked together out of the kitchen in the direction of the voices. It would be a busy night with a lot of people to feed, but Nadine sighed contentedly.

No matter what happened at dinner, Nadine was happy that she'd get to spend the evening with the people she cared about most in the world.

Chapter Seven

NADINE WALKED AROUND the sitting room with a tray of hors d'oeuvres, while the Farmhouse Inn's newest employee, Ivy Wood, set a tray of drinks on the small table between the large windows that boasted an expansive view of the property. Marian flitted between the kitchen and the crowd that had gathered near the fireplace, moving effortlessly in and out of conversation with her guests.

"Welcome to the Farmhouse Inn," she crowed to a handsome middle-aged couple dressed in tweed. Though their ensembles were a bit drab, Marian could see that they had taken care of themselves throughout the years. "I'm Marian Bright, owner and manager. I'm sorry I haven't gotten to meet you sooner. How are your accommodations?"

"Wonderful," the man enthused in a voice much deeper than Marian would have expected based on his lanky frame. "I'm Grant Hubley, and this is my wife, Louise."

"I'm so pleased to meet you, Louise," Marian said warmly and extended her hand to exchange a brief shake with the woman.

Louise accepted the gesture and, never taking her eyes off the floor, responded with a quiet "Likewise."

Her hand is like a dead fish, Marian thought but was careful not to let her smile slip.

"You'll have to forgive my wife," Grant said, leaning in as though sharing a secret. "She's terribly shy and meeting new people is never easy for her."

Marian turned her attention back to Louise and said, "While you're here, you can consider yourself among friends."

"Thank you," Mrs. Hubley murmured.

After a discreet glance around the room, Marian noticed a woman who appeared to be alone holding a glass of wine and staring out the window. This must be the cat lady, she noted.

With a quick "Excuse me," Marian disentangled herself from the Hubleys and made her way to the woman.

"Hello. I don't believe we've met. I'm Marian Bright, owner of the Farmhouse Inn."

The woman turned vacant eyes toward her and acknowledged Marian with a brief "Hello."

"I hope your room is suitable," she said, at a loss of anything else to say. Marian shook her head subtly. She was never at a loss for words, and the feeling was uncomfortable.

"Oh, yes. It's fine," the woman said absently.

Tough customer, Marian thought in dismay.

"May I ask your name?" she requested gently, mentally crossing her fingers that she wouldn't scare the woman off.

"Oh, uh, Cassandra. My name is Cassandra. Cassandra Weaver."

"It's so nice to meet you, Cassandra." Then, on a whim, Marian added, "Is everything okay, Cassandra?"

The woman took a sip of wine and said, "Of course. Why wouldn't it be?"

"Just checking. Now if you'll excuse me, I need to check on dinner," Marian said and rushed to the kitchen, not so much to check the food as to get away from the awkward woman. It was a rare person who wouldn't cooperate in making conversation with Marian.

Marian took a quick peek at the food so she wouldn't be lying, then went back to greet the last couple enjoying their pre-dinner cocktails.

She approached the man and woman, both looking like they were in their late twenties or early thirties and put on her gracious hostess face. "Hello, there. I'm Marian Bright, owner of the Farmhouse Inn. I don't believe we've had the chance to meet."

The woman spoke first. "I'm Chrissy Turner, and this is my husband, Wes."

"Hi," Wes grunted.

Nice guy, Marian thought sarcastically, but held the smile firmly on her face. "I'm so glad you chose to spend some time with us here at the bed-and-breakfast. How long are you planning to stay?"

"You're the owner, shouldn't you know that?" Wes observed in a brusque tone as Chrissy gave his shoulder a light smack.

"I'm sorry for Wes. Coming here was my idea. Pop-up community isn't his thing. To answer your question, we booked the room for two nights."

"It's no problem, and normally he'd be right, but for the past week or so I've been so busy that I haven't so much as answered the phone. You probably spoke to Nadine when you made reservations. That's her, carrying the tray of food," Marian said, pointing across the room to where Nadine was trying to coax the lonely looking Cassandra Weaver to eat something. Glancing at her watch, Marian realized it was only a few minutes until dinner would be served. She excused herself and crossed the room to Nadine, alerting her to the time, then the two of them went to the kitchen.

"It's a tough group out there," Nadine commented.

"No kidding. That Cassandra woman is like talking to a wall."

Nadine nodded in agreement. "She looked at me like I was trying to poison her with the hors d'oeuvres. She didn't have any problem with the wine, though. She probably drank three or four glasses."

"That would explain the empty look in her eyes. She was probably three sheets to the wind," Marian remarked, then got down to business. "I need you to help me carry the serving dishes to the table, then please gather everyone in the dining room. Hopefully the rest of our dinner guests will be here to help move the conversation along. We certainly can't count on that group of characters to have any interest in socializing, or even be capable of it, for that matter. Mr. Hubley and Chrissy Turner seem to be the only normal ones in the group." Marian hooked her thumb over her shoulder for emphasis.

Women on a mission to nourish their guests, Marian took the serving plates out of the warmer while Nadine garnished. As a team, they carried the food and placed it down the center of the table. Family-style meals always seemed like a good idea, but with the crowd tonight, Marian had a hunch that the only kind of family they would resemble is a dysfunctional one.

Chapter Eight

FRIENDLY CHATTER FILLED the dining room of the Farmhouse Inn Bed & Breakfast as the locals led the conversation. With all the charm of a born-and-bred Southern belle, Sylvia skillfully asked questions and offered information about herself and Saddle Hill to the guests of the inn.

"So you don't actually live here?" Wes Turner remarked after Sylvia mentioned her career in New York.

"Not full time, no, but Saddle Hill certainly feels like home. It has since the first time I set foot in this town," Sylvia said, a slight defensive edge to her voice. "Besides, I do have a house here, so I *am* an official resident." Her strained smile was the only indication that the rude guest had offended her.

"Must be nice to have enough money to have two houses," Wes snorted, then shoveled a bite of roast chicken into his mouth.

"So, where are you from?" Holly interjected, receiving a grateful nod from Sylvia.

This time, it was Wes's wife, Chrissy, who answered. "Oh,

here and there, really. We never stay in one place very long. Wes says the world is too big to be tied to one place." She placed a hand on her husband's forearm. "Isn't that right, sweetheart?"

"You bet your sweet—" Wes stopped, cleared his throat, then said, "Yes, that's right."

Patricia Jingle jumped in on the conversation with, "It must be so interesting to see so many places. We hardly get out of Saddle Hill, ourselves. Isn't that right, James?"

Quickly swallowing the food in his mouth, James patted his mouth with the cloth napkin that had been draped across his lap and nodded in agreement. "That's right. We've been so fortunate to live in the perfect town, I can't imagine why we'd ever leave."

"Not even to deliver your toys?" Wes mocked. The topic of the Jingle family's odd Christmas traditions had come up during cocktails, and it seemed as though Wes Turner wasn't going to miss an opportunity to poke fun at the Jingle family patriarch.

"Now, wait a second," Patricia snapped. "You don't even know my husband, and you have no right to make fun of him. I'll have you know that he's brought a lot of joy to people over the years, and that's more than a lot of people can say. You'll do well to watch what you say at this table."

James Jingle, though he had a reputation as having a short temper, merely patted Patricia's hand and crooned, "It's okay, dear. I've learned that you can't take everything so seriously. This young man clearly has his own opinions, and he's entitled to them."

With a final glare at the offending party, Patricia picked up her fork and plowed some potatoes into her mouth. As she chewed, she cast occasional glances at Wes Turner, who sat there with a self-satisfied smile on his face.

"So, Mr. and Mrs. Hubley," Eli Nolan said, taking control of the uncomfortable situation. "Tell us a little about yourselves."

Grant balanced his fork on the edge of his plate, took a sip of water from the goblet in front of him, and said, "Well, I've recently retired, so Louise and I are exploring different ways of living."

A chorus of voices from around the table joined in with, "Congratulations!"

"That's wonderful," Eli commented. "What did you do before retirement?"

"Actually, I was a college professor," he volunteered.

"Is that so?" Kris Jingle said, suddenly interested in the conversation.

"Yes, I taught English literature. And Louise, here, has been my rock through my whole career. I can't imagine myself being successful without her." He covered his wife's hand with his own and gave it a little squeeze. "Truth is, Louise has the patience of a saint."

"Wives have to. On the other hand, I have to say the same thing about my Roger. He had to put up with an awful lot from me," Marian joked as she entered the dining room with a pitcher of ice water. "Anybody need a refill?"

"I'll have some, please," Louise said in a mousy voice that certainly didn't sound like anyone's rock.

"Sure thing, darlin'," Marian chirped as she circled the table and refilled the water glass.

After placing the pitcher on the buffet, Marian pulled up a chair she kept in the corner of the room and settled into it between the Hubleys and Miss-No-Personality Cassandra Weaver.

"How about you?" Marian asked Cassandra. "What brings you here?"

The woman raised a shoulder and let it drop, staring down at her plate as she did. "I just needed to get away for a few days."

Sensing the woman wouldn't appreciate being pushed into further conversation, Marian said, "Well, I'm glad you chose our little slice of paradise for your getaway."

A noncommittal nod was Cassandra's only response.

"Okay, then," Marian said cheerfully. "I think I'll go help Ivy get dessert ready."

As Marian stood, Wes pushed his chair back and, with his hand under Chrissy's elbow, raised her with him as he stood. "None for us, please. I think we're going to call it a night. Thank you for a delicious meal."

Her face filled with confusion, Chrissy smiled and followed her husband out of the dining room.

"What a delightful man," Sylvia said, then rolled her eyes. "I don't understand what any woman would see in him. It was obvious his wife wasn't too keen on skipping out on dessert. How can she just let him boss her around like that?"

"It takes all kinds," Joe murmured. "I'll tell you this, though. Nadine, sweet as she is, would never put up with me acting like that."

"No, she wouldn't," Holly and Sylvia agreed in unison.

As Marian and Ivy slid the plates of apple pie à la mode in front of each dinner guest, Vito came in, dripping wet and short of breath. "I just heard on the news that the mayor has declared a state of emergency for Saddle Hill. Over the past hour, everything has iced over. It looks like everyone will be staying here tonight."

Chapter Nine

THE DINNER GUESTS began murmuring while Marian attempted to quiet them down.

"Everyone!" she said, clapping her hands. "There's no need to be upset. Why don't you all go to the sitting room and enjoy the fireplace. Ivy and I will bring your desserts and coffee to you there. Nadine, would you please help us?"

Nadine nodded and retreated to the kitchen with Ivy on her heels.

Reluctantly, each person scooted their chair back and stood, a look of uncertainty on their faces. Obviously when the guests checked in or made a reservation for dinner, they weren't planning on being stuck there.

Though she would never let on that she was concerned, Marian mentally ran through the contents of the pantry, refrigerator, and freezer, hoping she'd have enough food to feed everyone for the undetermined amount of time they'd all be there.

When she pushed open the door to the kitchen, Marian saw that Nadine and Ivy's thoughts mirrored her own.

"Do we have enough food for this?" Nadine worried aloud as she wrung her hands.

"Who will feed my dog and let her out to use the bathroom?" Ivy fretted.

Marian tsk-tsked at the younger women and, in the soothing tone of everyone's favorite grandmother-figure, said, "We can't worry our guests. Nadine, one thing I learned from growing up poor was how to stretch a meal to make it last." She turned toward Ivy, "Do you have a neighbor that would be willing to go over to your house to take care of your dog?"

The young woman thought for a moment. "Maybe. I'll need to make some calls."

"Good, but you better call before the ice knocks out the telephone line. While you get that settled, I need to get this pie out to our guests before the ice cream melts completely and makes the entire thing an inedible, mushy mess," Marian said.

As instructed, Nadine grabbed a large serving tray and gathered the plates filled with pie and rapidly melting ice cream while Ivy went to the office to make her call. After passing it out to the worried-looking guests, they went back to the dining room to retrieve coffee cups and a carafe of regular coffee and one of decaf. Marian mentally crossed her fingers that most of the diners would choose decaf. The last thing she needed was worried guests becoming more high-strung and unable to sleep.

❧

"I just can't believe we're going to be stuck here," Louise Hubley said in a tone that sounded more like whining than worrying.

Grant shook his head. "Louise, dear, we were planning to be here for a few nights, anyway. Nothing has changed."

"Yes, but now we don't have a choice. We *have* to stay here all the time instead of even having the option of going into town."

"Get a hold of yourself," he chided. "Everything is going to be just fine. We had no intention of leaving this place, anyway. After a rigorous career in academia, a quiet country escape is just what I need. Besides, it's not like we'll be here the rest of our lives. The roads will be cleared and we'll be on our way, just as we planned."

Louise shrugged in response to her husband's assurances. He was never one to worry. That was her job. He just lived in his ivory tower and left the details to her.

"He's right, you know," Joe interjected over a mouthful of apple pie from his seat in the corner of the room. "Even though we're in a remote part of town, our road crews are top-notch. They're used to unpredictable weather and will have us out of here in no time."

"Except that you were almost killed coming out to this place last year when we had snow and ice," Holly muttered, casting a pained, sideways glance at her new husband. After all the disappointment in her life, she still hadn't shaken the fear of losing Eli and her friends after they were in that accident last year.

"We weren't almost killed," Eli corrected. "We slid off the road. That was all."

"You had a nasty concussion," Holly countered, "and it could have been much worse."

"But it wasn't."

"Well, what matters is that we're all safe and sound and we got Marian back before it was too late," Sylvia interjected, her voice cheery, even if it was a little forced. "Now look. We're all together in this amazing farmhouse. We're warm and have food to eat. We're lucky."

The flames crackled in the fireplace as each of the guests sipped their coffee. The heat was extra comforting as the ice pelted against the windows and the wind howled through the trees outside.

Marian walked around with the carafe of coffee, refilling or topping the cups off for anyone who wanted more. "Well, we can certainly count our blessings that we're safe and secure in here. A year ago, I wouldn't have been able to say that, but Vito has done marvelous work getting this place shipshape."

From the corner of her eye, Marian noticed a slight pink shade creep up Sylvia's neck. Apparently Vito wasn't the only one that was smitten. She smiled to herself and offered more decaf to Grant and Louise Hubley.

"No thanks," Louise said. "I think we'll turn in. We'll see you all in the morning, I suppose. What time is breakfast?"

"Nine o'clock," Marian said. "I'll ring a bell to give everyone a ten-minute warning."

"Excellent! Good night, all," Grant said heartily as he placed a hand under Louise's elbow and guided her out of the sitting room and down the hall to their suite.

"I think I'll retire as well," Cassandra announced, reminding everyone that she was still there. Though she didn't participate in the conversation and almost everyone probably forgot she was even in the room, it seemed odd that she felt the need to call attention to the fact that she was leaving.

"G'night," the remaining group called after her as she disappeared from the room.

"Now, that's a strange lady," Joe mumbled when she was out of earshot.

Once the strangers were gone, the group of friends sat quietly around the fire.

"I hate to bring this up, but if we're not allowed to leave, where are we supposed to sleep?" Holly asked Marian.

Marian chewed on her lip a moment as she thought, then said, "With me. The girls, anyway. Vito did a magnificent job converting the old barn into a duplex. The fellas will stay with him on his side, and the girls will stay with me on my side," she said firmly, leaving no room for discussion.

Since Vito and Marian both lived on the property and shared the barn-turned-duplex, and because all the rooms in the farmhouse were occupied, it was the only option available.

As the group helped tidy up and wash the dishes, the thought in each one's mind was that, with this crew of guests, the next few days could be very interesting.

Chapter Ten

MARIAN CARRIED HER own cup of coffee and took a seat in one of the chairs around the fireplace. Heaving a deep sigh, she raised the cup to her lips and took a long sip.

"Marian, you outdid yourself with that roast chicken," Eli said as he leaned back into the plush sofa cushions.

"And that pie!" Sylvia chimed in. "I'm going to need bigger pants."

"Oh, go on," Marian said, dismissing the compliments. "These are the dishes I've made for years and you've had dozens of times. The only difference now is that I'm making them for a whole lot more people."

"We had a good crew for dinner tonight," Nadine observed. "Looks like the same ones will be here for breakfast. And lunch. And dinner again tomorrow."

Marian blew out a puff of air toward the short, wavy hair resting on her forehead. "And for the foreseeable future, apparently. Vito?" She turned and faced the back of the room where he stood off from the group. "Come here and tell us everything you heard on the radio."

Vito cleared his throat and took several steps forward. "I just heard that the roads are treacherous, especially out here away from town. Mayor Roswell declared a state of emergency and urged everyone to stay where they are and not attempt to drive on the ice."

"For how long?" Joe grumbled, clearly unhappy to be trapped away from home and the station. As sheriff, he took his role very seriously and didn't want anything to get in the way of his duty to uphold justice.

Vito shrugged in response. "No idea. According to the weather station, it's supposed to be like this for the next couple days. I'd say we'll all be staying put for at least forty-eight hours. Maybe seventy-two."

"At least we're with people we like," Holly said. Her state of newlywed bliss kept her head in the clouds. Everyone there knew that as long as she was with Eli, she'd be content no matter the situation.

Nadine chuckled. "That's true for us, anyway. I'm not so sure the others will be terribly happy to be stuck here. Especially that Wes character. He didn't seem happy to be here in the first place. Wait till he finds out he can't go anywhere. At least his wife seems nice."

"Do we have somebody that's gonna be trouble?" Vito asked, his eyes darkening.

"Ever the protector," Sylvia said through a smile.

A shade that settled somewhere between red and pink crept up Vito's neck and spread onto his square jaw. "Habit," he mumbled.

Sylvia dropped her gaze then looked up at him through her dark lashes. "I was just kidding."

Silence fell over the group as they observed the interaction between Vito and Sylvia. They all knew that Vito had been sweet on her for the better part of a year, and the smiles that tugged on the corners of their mouths communicated that they just realized the feeling was mutual.

Breaking the silence, Marian interjected, "Well, I'm mighty glad Vito has been around this past year to be my protector. He's been a great partner here at the B&B, *and* a great neighbor."

"Speaking of neighbor," Kris said, obviously annoyed, "am I allowed to ask how we're all supposed to cram into your duplex while we're stuck here?" It seemed as though tonight he'd earned the nickname they'd given him behind his back several months ago.

Curmudgeonly Kris.

"Like I said before, the ladies are more than welcome to stay with me. I have plenty of room. When Vito renovated that old barn into our duplex, he gave us each four bedrooms. What he thought we needed with four bedrooms, I don't know, but they'll certainly come in handy right now. We might need to pull out some sleeping bags and air mattresses for you guys, though. I've seen Vito's place and, well, it's a bit sparse."

A few soft chuckles rippled through the small crowd, and Sylvia said, "Thank you, Marian. It can be like a grown-up slumber party."

"No pillow fights, though," Marian warned. "We can't afford to have anyone get hurt when we can't get you to the doctor."

"Fair enough," Nadine agreed with a small giggle.

The corner of Kris's mouth drooped further into a frown. "Sleeping bags?"

Marian ignored him and cast a glance toward Vito. "Any objection to the guys staying with you?"

"No problem at all," Vito agreed. "Even though some of you will have to sleep on air mattresses on the floor, we can treat it like a campout."

"Son, I haven't been on a campout since 1975," James Jingle said in his usually jolly tone. He patted his round belly. "If I get down on the floor, I might never be able to get up."

"We'll hoist you," Joe remarked with a grin.

Nadine stood and began gathering dishes. "I'll clean up, then I think we should brave the ice to walk out to the barn."

"We'll help," Holly and Sylvia said in unison. The two women joined her and began shuttling dishes into the kitchen. Patricia, Ivy, and Marian followed suit. Soon, the dishes were washed and put away and everyone was bundling up in their jackets, hats, gloves, and scarves.

Through the glass in the back door, the ice on the ground shimmered like diamonds in the light from the porch.

"Everyone be careful," Marian warned as they opened the back door.

Just before the group was about to begin filing out of the house, a scream from the direction of the sitting room made them all stop in their tracks.

Marian, a worried look on her otherwise cheerful face, turned and darted in the direction of the voice. Joe, a sheriff to his core, followed close behind with Eli hot on his heels.

They burst through the door from the kitchen and Marian, slightly out of breath, gasped, "What's wrong?"

A trembling Louise Hubley stood by the still-warm fireplace with her fingertips pressed to her lips. Finally, with tears in her eyes, she choked out, "We've been robbed!"

Chapter Eleven

MARIAN DRAPED A blanket over Louise Hubley's shoulders then settled in next to the trembling woman.

"Drink this," Nadine said as she placed a cup of decaf in Louise's shaking hands.

"Tell us what happened," Marian urged gently.

Louise took a sip of the coffee. The crowd that had been about to go out to the duplex had shrugged off their winter coats and hats and was now gathered around the visibly shaken robbery victim in the sitting room.

"I just…I don't know. I don't know where to start," Louise stammered. Silence followed as the group waited for Louise to speak.

"Why don't you begin by telling us what happened when you went back to your room," Joe encouraged. As the town's sheriff, he was used to questioning victims and perpetrators. Once known for being brusque and quick-tempered, the past several months as a father had mellowed him, and it showed in his softer approach with Louise.

Mrs. Hubley brought the cup of coffee to her lips and took a slow drink. The shaking of her hands had lessened, a good sign as far as Marian was concerned.

"When Grant and I got back to our room, we noticed that some things had been moved around. I had a small travel jewelry case on my nightstand, and I noticed it was missing. I searched everywhere I could think of in that room but didn't find it." She paused as a tear squeezed out of the corner of her eye and rolled down her cheek. "The earrings Grant bought me for our first wedding anniversary were in there," she said as a sob choked out of her throat.

"Where is your husband now?" Joe asked.

"He's doing an inventory of our other things to make sure nothing else is missing. He's a very detail-oriented person." Then Louise added, almost as an afterthought, "It served him well in academia."

Marian clasped Louise's slender hand in her own. "I'm sure it did. I think I'll go check on him." As she rose from her spot next to the woman, Marian whispered to Joe as she passed him, "With the road conditions being what they are, I doubt any-body broke in, and it's not likely that anyone would have been able to leave even if they did manage to get in here. We need to do a thorough search of the premises."

The corner of Joe's mouth curved in an amused smile. "Will do, chief."

Marian smiled back and shook her head. "Would you listen to me? I helped solve one crime two years ago and now I'm acting like an old pro. Of course, you know how to do your job. I'm sorry for implying otherwise."

"No apology necessary," he said to her retreating back as she walked in the direction of the Hubleys' garden-view room. Turning his attention back to the robbery victim, he said, "Usually I'd get your statement down at the station, but since we're not likely to get there in the near future, we'll need to do it here." He looked at his wife of almost two years. "Nay, would you get me some paper and something to write with?"

Nadine nodded in the affirmative and walked toward the small office she and Marian shared behind the kitchen.

"Eli," Joe said, turning his attention back toward his deputy, "I'd like you to go check on the other guests and make sure nothing else is missing."

"Sure thing, boss," Eli said, then hoisted himself from the cushy chair he'd been sitting in and dropped a kiss on Holly's forehead. "That's my cue. Why don't you go on to Marian's and I'll pop in to see you before I go to bed?"

Holly nodded in agreement. "Be careful," she whispered.

"I will, but there's no danger here," Eli assured his wife.

"Okay," she said uncertainly, then watched as he turned and walked toward the bedrooms.

"Can I get you anything else?" Nadine offered their shaken guest while keeping a concerned eye on her friend. "Another piece of pie, maybe?"

"Oh, no dear. I couldn't possibly eat at a time like this. The coffee was just what I needed to take the chill off. I think I must have gone into partial shock."

Patting the woman's shoulder, Marian sighed. "Anybody would, I suppose. I'm so sorry this happened to you while you were staying at my establishment. I assure you I'll do whatever I can to make it right."

A small smile tugged at Louise's lips. "Thank you. That's very kind, but this isn't your fault." Then looking far off into the distance, she muttered, "I've never been robbed before. I can't say I care for it."

"Who would?" Vito chimed in from the corner.

Joe cleared his throat. "Mrs. Hubley, why don't you and I go to the dining room where I can get your official statement. We'll have your husband join us shortly."

Nodding in agreement at his request, Louise placed the coffee cup on the small end table to the left of the sofa and stood. "Maybe talking about it will jog my memory about who could be responsible for such a heinous act."

Joe led the way, and Louise followed, casting a last glance at the group and forcing a smile at the small group.

When they were safely out of earshot, Holly whispered, "The thief has to be someone here at the bed-and-breakfast."

Sylvia nodded thoughtfully. "I thought the same thing. The question is, who is it?"

Chapter Twelve

ELI ALREADY KNEW that none of the Saddle Hill residents was responsible for the robbery, and the only other people there were a couple that didn't seem very interested in socializing, a middle-aged woman who might have a few screws loose but otherwise seemed harmless, and the retired professor and his wife, who were the victims.

Shaking his head, he made his way to the largest suite where the Turners were staying. That Wes character seemed like a real piece of work. Angry and snide, he was obviously not there to make friends with the other guests. His wife, on the other hand, seemed more civilized.

Wonder what his problem is, Eli thought as he raised his hand to knock on the door of their suite. His knuckles rapped on the wood in a loud thud. He lowered his hand and waited.

No answer.

He knocked again, louder this time.

Still nothing.

Pressing his ear against the door and straining to hear

any sound coming from inside, he frowned. Maybe they were already asleep and were wearing earplugs, he thought.

Despite the gnawing in his gut, he decided to try again later and walked a few doors down to Cassandra Weaver's room. After knocking loudly, he put his ear against the door in time to hear a hurried, scuffling sound coming from the room. Some drawers and doors slammed, followed by muffled cursing and heavy footsteps coming in his direction.

"Wonder what's up with her," Eli muttered to himself just before the door was yanked open.

"Yes? What do you want?" the woman demanded, her cheeks red and her breath coming quicker than a trip across the room should warrant.

"Are you okay, ma'am?"

"Of course I am," she snapped. "Why wouldn't I be? I was just getting ready to get in the shower when you interrupted me."

"I'm very sorry about that Ms.—"

"Weaver. My last name is Weaver," Cassandra cut in before Eli could finish.

"Well, Ms. Weaver, I'm very sorry to interrupt, but we've had a complaint that someone's valuables have gone missing, and I wanted to make sure you—"

"I didn't take anything," Cassandra said quickly.

"I didn't say you did," Eli said calmly. "If you had let me finish my sentence, you would have heard me say that I wanted to make sure you were okay."

Laughing nervously, she glanced quickly over her shoulder and said, "Of course. Where are my manners? Sometimes a woman traveling alone has to be diligent in making sure trouble doesn't find her. I hope you'll forgive me."

Eli stole a quick look over her shoulder, following the line of vision where she'd glanced just moments earlier.

There's something she doesn't want me to see, he thought, using all his effort to keep his face fixed in a neutral expression.

"Ma'am, are you alone in here?" Eli asked, cocking an inquisitive eyebrow.

"Of course I am," Cassandra replied through nervous laughter. "Who would be in here with me? I checked in alone."

Eli narrowed his eyes at the woman. She was hiding something, but he had nothing but his gut to go on. "Well, please let us know if you have any concerns while you're here." He took a card from his breast pocket and handed it to her. "Call this number if you need anything."

The nervous laughter over, the sour expression on her face returned. "The only thing I need is for people to leave me alone. I came here to relax, not to be hassled by local law enforcement."

Eli's head jerked as if she'd slapped him, and he couldn't help but wonder where the sudden change in mood came from. His back stiffened at the accusation, but he held his tongue. "Well, if we can be of assistance, please don't hesitate to let us know. Since it appears that we're all stuck here for the foreseeable future, I'm sure we'll be seeing a lot of each other."

"Not if I can help it," the bitter woman retorted, then went back into her room and slammed the door.

With that he sighed, turned, and went to the next room— the one the Hubleys were staying in. He hoped Mr. Hubley would have more decency than Ms. Cassandra Weaver did. If not, he'd content himself with leaving this theft unsolved.

Across the hall, in the suite with the garden view, was Grant Hubley. Eli knocked more gently than he had for the other two rooms and was greeted with the grim face of the retired professor.

"I'm sorry to bother you," Eli apologized when the door swung open. "I just wanted to check on you and make sure you were okay and to see if you've discovered that anything else is missing."

Grant raked a hand through his salt-and-pepper hair and stepped out of the way so Eli could enter the room. "As you can see, the mess in here is making it a little harder to take inventory, but I'm managing," he said as he waved a hand around the ransacked room. "How's Louise?"

"She seems shaken, but okay," Eli replied. "She's talking with Sheriff Adler right now. Marian and the rest of them are taking good care of her. A cup of decaf seems to have slowed the shaking."

The professor shook his head slowly. "I feel like I should be with her. Louise is very sentimental. Some of the jewelry I've gotten for her throughout our relationship is what has been stolen. There was one pair of earrings that she's especially upset about. I tried to tell her it's just stuff and that nothing she lost can't be replaced, but she won't listen."

"I guess this is one of the differences between men and women," Eli agreed. "Holly has a whole box of things from ticket stubs to candy wrappers that remind her of when we were dating. I look at it and see a box of trash."

Mr. Hubley nodded his head knowingly. "Jewelry is more valuable than scraps of paper, but I suppose it represents the same sentimentality." He paused, glancing around the room. "If you don't mind, I'd like to finish going through our things and then get the place tidied up before Louise gets back. I don't think seeing that the place is still a mess will do her any favors. She's the high-strung type and needs things to be a certain way."

"Of course," Eli agreed. "Normally we'd have to lock this place down as a crime scene, but considering the weather and the condition of the roads, it's safe to say that whoever took your wife's jewelry is still here. We'll find it."

"I hope so," Grant sighed. "I hate to see my wife unhappy."

"I understand. Please let us know if you need anything. With all of us being stuck here together for the time being, I'm sure we'll be seeing a lot of each other."

"I'm sure," the professor muttered, then turned back to his task.

Leaving the room quietly, Eli clicked the door closed behind him and went back down the hall to the Turners' suite. He knocked again, hoping this time someone would answer the door.

When he'd knocked several more times with no answer, the gnawing feeling in Eli's stomach grew.

If he didn't know any better, he'd think something had happened to the young couple with the friendly wife and the surly husband.

Chapter Thirteen

NADINE SCRUBBED A nonexistent stain on the counter and sighed. This was going to be a long couple of days. Even though she was used to bringing Josephine to work with her, she never thought she'd have to pack enough baby supplies to last days. She had enough diapers to last about a day, but that was it. What would she do after tomorrow if they were still stuck there?

If the weather didn't make things bad enough, now there'd been a theft that would occupy Joe's time and attention. Without his usual resources, it would be a lot harder to solve the case. It was no doubt that the crime scene had already been compromised, which would make lifting fingerprints nearly impossible.

Add to that the fact that she had to stay in Marian's half of the duplex with a baby that still wasn't sleeping through the night and would likely keep everyone else awake, Nadine's stress level was a lot higher than it should be considering she got to spend a few days in a relaxing place with her closest friends.

Someone cleared their throat behind her, and Nadine turned to see Holly and Sylvia standing shoulder-to-shoulder, watching her wipe the counter.

"Think it's clean yet?" Sylvia remarked, an amused smirk on her face.

"Oh, uh, I was just thinking," Nadine stammered, then tossed the washcloth into the sink. "It's going to be a rough couple of days, I'm afraid."

Holly shrugged. "Maybe. It could be a lot of fun, though. Didn't you ever dream of getting snowed in as a kid? I always wanted to get stuck in a cabin with people I love. This is pretty close, I'd say."

"Yeah, except I have a duty to the guests to make their stay as pleasant as possible. That will be pretty hard when the weather is terrible, I have no clothes to change into, and we've already had a theft." Nadine's face twisted into a grimace. "How am I supposed to handle all that?"

Sylvia took a few steps toward her friend and wrapped Nadine in a tight hug. "You're not alone in this," she soothed. "In fact, you're not even the one in charge. Marian will take care of the guests. You know that. Joe and Eli will figure out who stole Mrs. Hubley's jewelry. This is not your weight to carry."

A tear trickled down Nadine's cheek and absorbed into Sylvia's sweater. "I know, but I need to do all this and still take care of Josephine. Joe will be preoccupied with the theft, but how will he solve it?"

Sylvia made quiet shushing sounds in Nadine's ear and said softly, "Good thing Josephine has her Aunt Sylvia and Aunt Holly here to help keep an eye on her."

Holly stepped toward the duo and put a hand on Nadine's

shoulder. "That's right. We'll get some quality time with our favorite girl while you do your thing to keep the guests satisfied. And don't worry about Joe. He has Eli, and between the two of them they'll figure this out. Besides, it should be easier to figure out who is responsible since no one can leave. The thief is stuck here." She wrapped her arms around her two friends and the three of them laughed together while Nadine wiped the tears from her cheeks.

The sound of the door to the kitchen slamming open made the three women step away from each other and turn to face the person who'd just rushed in.

"Is Joe still with Mrs. Hubley?" Eli said, his face flushed pink.

"I think so," Holly confirmed. "What's wrong?"

"It's the Turners," Eli said, his eyes darting around the kitchen, searching for nothing in particular.

"What about them?" Nadine asked, her eyebrows furrowed in a frown. "Are they okay?"

Eli looked from woman to woman, his focus finally settling on Nadine. "They're not in their room. I think they've flown the coop."

✥

Holly and Sylvia exchanged glances as Nadine held Eli's gaze.

"Flown the coop? You mean they're gone?" Nadine clarified.

Eli nodded and licked his lips. "You got anything to drink?"

Holly rushed to fill a glass with water and handed it to her new husband. She took his elbow and led him to a stool at the counter. "Sit," she commanded as he slid onto the seat. "Tell us what happened."

Eli took a long drink of the water and set it down on the counter with a clank. "I should probably talk to Joe about this first."

"Hold on," Sylvia said, placing a restraining hand on Eli's shoulder when he started to stand. "What makes you think they're gone?"

Eli picked up the glass and took another long drink. "I went to each of the guests' rooms to find out if they'd seen anything," he said when he lowered the glass. "Mr. Hubley was more than willing to talk. I mean, of course he was. It was his room that had been robbed. Cassandra Weaver seemed much more nervous about me 'snooping' around, as she called it," he said as he hooked his fingers into air quotes. "I don't know if it's because I'm law enforcement, or because I'm a man, or just because she's awkward, but she seemed really uncomfortable that I was there."

Nadine squeezed the bridge of her nose where she felt a headache beginning. "What does this have to do with the Turners? Why do you think they're gone?"

"Oh, right. The Turners," Eli said almost absently. "When I knocked on their door, no one answered. I moved on to Ms. Weaver's room. I figured maybe someone was in the shower, or maybe wearing earplugs, so I went back when I had finished talking to Ms. Weaver. I knocked again, harder this time so I could be sure someone heard me, even if they were sleeping or wearing earplugs or were in the shower. There was still no answer. The only possible reason for them not to answer is because they were gone."

Nadine nodded and chewed her lip. "Marian has a key to each of the rooms. I think you need to talk to Joe about your suspicions, and if he thinks you all need to get in, we can open the door for you," she offered.

"I'll go talk to him now," Eli said, standing from his seat at the counter and quickly walked from the kitchen toward the dining room.

"If the roads are so bad, they can't be gone," Nadine said, turning to face Holly and Sylvia. "Right?"

Chapter Fourteen

"ANYTHING?" ELI ASKED Joe after Louise Hubley returned to her room.

Joe stood from his chair at the dining room table and stretched his back. "Not really. She certainly seems the nervous type, but I don't think she's making this up. We have no reason to doubt that her jewelry really is missing."

Eli frowned and settled into a chair across the table from the one Joe had just vacated. "I hadn't even considered the possibility that she was imagining it. It just never occurred to me."

"Well, that doesn't seem to be the case, so don't beat yourself up over it," Joe said, then plopped back into the chair. "Were you able to talk to the other guests?"

Eli snorted. "For the most part, yes. Grant Hubley didn't seem to have anything to hide. He was by far the most open with me, but that could be because his wife was the victim. He was busy cleaning the room. Trying to get it to look normal for when she came back, I guess."

Joe scratched the stubble on his chin. "I wish we had been

able to search the room before he contaminated the crime scene."

Raising a shoulder and letting it drop, Eli said, "We probably shouldn't have let him go back to the room. This is certainly not the kind of crime we're used to."

Joe shook his head thoughtfully. "What about the other guests? Did you get anything from them?"

Eli shifted in his seat. "Well, that Cassandra Weaver is one strange lady, I'll tell you that. She's got a few squirrels in her attic, if you get my drift. She kept acting like I was interrupting something, and she kept looking behind her like there was someone else in the room. Let's just say she wasn't too happy that I interrupted whatever she was in the middle of. She said I was 'hassling' her." The deputy rolled his eyes. "Since when is asking if someone heard or saw anything pertaining to a theft 'hassling'?"

"Weird," Joe muttered. "Marian said she checked in alone. We could see that the woman was just plain odd during dinner, though. And what about that other couple? The Turners? I think that's their last name."

Running his fingers nervously through his hair, Eli said, "Well, I didn't actually get a chance to talk to them."

In a reflexive move, Joe banged the table with the palm of his hand. "What do you mean you didn't get a chance to talk to them? Why not?"

"Well, uh, it's just that…" Eli stammered.

"It's just that what?" Joe's impatience was growing by the second. Gone was the newer, more mellow version of the sheriff.

"Well, they uh, they didn't answer their door."

"Did you try knocking louder?"

Eli's nervousness vanished and was replaced by irritation. "Of course, I did. I'm not an idiot."

"How about trying again? Did you try again?"

"Of course. Like I said, I'm not an idiot," Eli said, annoyance evident in his words.

"No, you're not," Joe said sheepishly. "I'm sorry. Tell me what happened."

Launching into his account with Cassandra Weaver and his failed attempts at talking to the Turners, Eli concluded with, "My gut is telling me they're gone."

Joe's mouth dropped open slightly before he spoke. "What do you mean they might be gone? Look outside. It's treacherous out there. Mayor Roswell has issued a state of emergency and told everyone to stay put. It would be ludicrous to be on the roads tonight."

"If they're the thieves, I don't think they'd let a little thing like an ice storm stand in the way of escaping with valuable jewelry," Eli said.

Joe seemed to consider Eli's logic for a minute. "It would make sense that the people responsible for the crime would try to get away before the weather conditions got even worse." He scratched his chin again, then made eye contact with his deputy. "Are we ready to say Wes and Chrissy Turner are the most likely suspects?"

Eli shrugged. "I think we should knock on their door again, and if there's no answer, get Marian to use the master key to let us into their room. If they're gone, then I think they have to be suspects. Why else would they leave in this weather without letting Marian or anyone else know?"

Joe's lips pursed in thought. "Good point. Let's go."

The two men slid their chairs back from the table and turned toward the hall leading to the guest suites. In a matter of minutes, they'd know if they had a suspect for the robbery at the Farmhouse Inn Bed & Breakfast.

Chapter Fifteen

MARIAN BUSTLED AROUND the kitchen, tidying the things that had already been tidied and wiping down the already spotless counters and cabinets. As she scrubbed the imaginary dirt, Holly sat on a stool in the corner of the kitchen watching the older woman with a mixture of amusement and annoyance.

"That stuff is already clean. Nadine did the same thing a little while ago. What's the point in cleaning it again?" Holly asked, a note of disdain in her voice.

Dropping the washcloth on the counter, Marian turned to face Holly and placed her hands on her hips. "It gives me something to do. 'Idle hands' and all that. There was a theft at my bed-and-breakfast, and I'm worried. I need something to occupy myself. There's no harm in things being extra clean," Marian retorted, then turned and picked up the washcloth and carried it to the sink where she rinsed it, wrung it out, and hung it over the edge of the sink to dry.

Holly studied Marian. "I don't think I've ever seen you this worried," the younger woman observed.

Marian ran her hands over her eyes and through her gray hair. "I admit that I am worried. A guest being robbed isn't exactly a great advertisement for the inn. Word gets out, and I'm sure I'll lose future business because of this."

Standing from her seat in the corner of the kitchen, Holly walked over to the woman she thought of as a grandmother and pulled her into a tight embrace. Marian's birdlike frame was slender and felt almost frail as Holly hugged her. She might have been worried if she didn't know that Marian was unusually strong for her size.

Returning the hug, the tiny woman sighed on Holly's shoulder. "Thank you, dear. I needed that," she murmured as she pulled away. "I know I'm thinking of the worst-case scenario here, and that short of doing background checks and fingerprinting my guests, there was nothing I could do to prevent it from happening. I know it's not my fault, but I still feel responsible."

"The only thing you're responsible for is cooking a fantastic dinner and making everyone feel welcome. Especially tonight, when we're all stuck here together and you've been gracious enough to open your home to the whole lot of us." Holly squeezed Marian's hand and looked directly into her eyes. "You're not to blame for anything bad that happened here tonight. In fact, I doubt you've done anything but bring good to people your entire life."

Marian returned the hand-squeeze. "Thank you, dear. You've brought a lot of good as well." She didn't mention the not-so-good things Holly brought to Saddle Hill two years ago when she first arrived, including a police record for shoplifting.

The tender moment was broken when Joe and Eli pushed open the swinging door that led from the dining room to the kitchen. Noting their grim faces, a lump settled in Marian's chest. "What's going on?" she asked, though she wasn't certain she wanted to know the answer.

Joe's mouth formed a grim line. "I need your master key to get into the Turners' room. They aren't answering their door."

"Maybe they're heavy sleepers. Or in the bathroom," Marian said hopefully, but the protest died on her lips as Eli shook his head.

"I've knocked on their door several times, and I haven't heard a single sound coming from that room. We need to get in there and check on them," Eli countered.

Marian sighed, then pulled a key ring from the pocket of her apron. Selecting a key color-coded in purple, she extended it toward Joe. "Please knock again before you go barging in there," she requested. "If they're just sleeping, this is going to be embarrassing for you, them, and me. I don't need reviews saying I allowed cops to bust into my guests' rooms and scare the daylights out of them."

"We will be discreet," Joe promised as he accepted the key ring. "But I don't think you have anything to worry about, except maybe the fact that one of your guests took off after something was stolen from another one."

The sinking feeling Marian had that began when Louise Hubley came in screaming about a theft only grew as the sheriff spoke. How was it possible that there could be a thief staying at her bed-and-breakfast?

"Please don't draw attention to yourselves," Marian requested as the two men disappeared from the kitchen. With a sigh, she plopped onto one of the stools at the counter and blew a wisp of hair out of her eyes.

"What if they really did it and flew the coop?" she asked Holly.

Holly shrugged in response. "I don't know, Marian, but what I do know is that everything will be okay. Eli and Joe will get everything sorted out."

Marian nodded in agreement. "You're right. They're good at their jobs."

"When they get back with your key, how about we head to bed? If we're going to be hosting everyone all day, it will take a lot of work and we'll need some rest," Holly suggested.

Just as Marian was about to concede, a grim-faced Joe Adler came back into the kitchen and returned Marian's key ring.

An icy lump sank to the pit of the older woman's stomach. "What did you find?" she asked, bracing herself for the worst.

Joe shook his head and said in a weary voice, "Eli was right. They're gone."

Chapter Sixteen

"YOU GIRLS GO ahead and go to bed," Marian ordered as she dangled the keys to her house in front of Holly, Nadine, and Sylvia.

"But there's a thief running around here somewhere. I think we need to stay and help figure out who it is," Holly protested, despite her suggestion mere minutes ago that they all go to bed.

"Joe and Eli are questioning our guests. You don't have anything to do. Get some rest," Marian said, her tone a little firmer than it had been.

Nadine, thinking better of arguing, reached out and accepted the keys Marian offered. "You don't have to tell me twice. I'm beat. It's been a long day. Besides, I need to get Josephine settled for the night. Assuming she's in the mood to sleep, that is."

Relinquishing the keys into Nadine's grasp, Marian smiled. "At least one of you has some sense," she teased, casting a look at Holly, who was like a granddaughter to her.

"You don't need to tell me twice, either," Sylvia said. "As

I've gotten older, I've realized just how important a good night's sleep is to me."

"Good," Marian said with a smile, then became serious. "Now, make sure you bundle up when you go out there. I think the ice is still coming down. Bundle little Josephine up, too. Such a tiny child shouldn't be exposed to this weather."

"Yes, ma'am," Nadine replied. Her own parents had died several years ago, and she was so glad her daughter had a surrogate grandmother like Marian. With a twinge of guilt, she admitted to herself that her own mother couldn't have been a better grandmother to Josie.

"I'll take good care of them," Sylvia said, slipping an arm around Nadine's shoulders. "Cross my heart."

Marian pulled both women into a tight hug. "Nighty night, girls. Make yourselves at home, and I'll try not to wake you when I come in."

Nadine and Sylvia returned the hug. "Thanks for letting us crash at your place till the weather clears," Sylvia remarked. "It sure beats trying to get home and getting ourselves killed on the way."

With a final squeeze, the two released the older woman and left the kitchen to gather the baby and their few belongings.

Though they were glad to have a place to stay during this most recent winter storm, as they walked to Marian's house, their feet crunching the ice-covered grass and the baby wrapped in a thick blanket, both Nadine and Sylvia were lost in their own thoughts.

If the past two Christmases were any kind of indicator, the theft at the bed-and-breakfast was likely to become a bigger problem than any of them cared to deal with.

Chapter Seventeen

J AMES AND PATRICIA Jingle sat on the covered porch of the duplex, chairs against the wall, with blankets wrapped around their shoulders. Nobody else had left the farmhouse yet, giving them a few minutes alone to enjoy the quiet and each other.

"The weather sure is wild tonight," James observed, his breath coming out in clouds of vapor as he spoke. Ice pinged off the metal roof as if to emphasize his statement.

Patricia nodded in agreement. "It sure is. If we have to be stuck somewhere other than home, though, this is a nice place to be."

James grunted. "Maybe for you. I'll be sleeping on an air mattress in a sleeping bag like I'm some boy scout on an indoor camping trip. I'm too old for this. They'll have to hoist me off the floor and I'd put money on my back hurting so much in the morning I can hardly walk," he grumbled.

Patricia laughed softly. "Oh, James. You'll be okay. Try not to be grouchy to the other guys, or you might not get invited on another camping trip." The wrinkles around Patricia's eyes deepened with her smile and her eyes danced with merriment.

James turned his head toward her, fully intending a retort, but the words died on his lips. "You really are beautiful, you know that, Patty?"

Her smile grew. "I'm glad you think so, even after all these years."

"You're a keeper, even though you're always trying to keep me in line."

She cocked an eyebrow at him. "Try? I'd say my success rate is pretty staggering, wouldn't you?"

"Yeah, yeah," James said, trying to hide his own smile.

Growing serious, Patricia said, "I'm sorry that awful young man made fun of you at dinner. He needs to learn some manners."

"It's okay, Patty. I've come to accept that my previous life might be viewed as strange to some folks. You taught me that I can't control another person's attitude, but I can control how I react to it," James remarked. "And you're right. Even as jolly as I was playing Santa, I'm happier and more at peace now."

Patricia reached out and stroked James's beard with the backs of her gloved fingers. "I'm glad."

"You know, this is the first time we'll be spending the night apart since we got married. Forty years and I haven't slept alone in all that time."

She let her hand drop. "I know… I hope the guys can handle your snoring."

James gave Patricia a playful shove, then clasped her hand in his own. "It's getting awfully cold sitting out here. Why don't you go on inside and warm up," he suggested.

"That's probably a good idea. I should claim my bed before everybody else gets here. You might want to do the same thing. With your air mattress and sleeping bag, I mean." Patricia winked at him, then leaned over to kiss his bearded cheek. "Goodnight, Mr. Claus."

"Goodnight, Mrs. Claus," James replied. "I'm going to sit here for another few minutes, then I'll head inside."

As James watched his wife walk inside, he reveled in his good luck that he'd found such a spunky and patient woman to marry. Many times over the past couple of years he'd wondered how she managed to stick it out with him for so long. Though he hadn't known it before, he'd become aware that he wasn't the easiest person to live with. For decades she'd played the part of Mrs. Claus without complaint, even though she'd tired of it long ago. When he told her she was a keeper, he meant it.

Sadly, he wondered if his sons would ever know the kind of happiness he'd found with their mother. Now divorced, Nicholas had been sitting in jail the past two years for stealing from Ralph Stockton's jewelry store and had another year to go on his sentence before he'd be released.

Nicholas—the son he had high hopes for—was a convicted criminal.

Then there was Kris. Poor Kris, who to James's knowledge had never been happy. He was miserable growing up in a house that celebrated Christmas year-round and felt like an outcast his whole life. He came close to being happy last year when he dated that reporter, Carol Ling. Though James didn't care for her, he did feel bad for his son when it turned out that she was the mastermind behind Marian's kidnapping last Christmas.

James sighed. Life had been easy for him the past forty years, and it was all because Patricia had made it that way. He could only pray that there was a woman out there who could do the same for Kris.

Chapter Eighteen

J OE SAT AT the kitchen island, his elbows propped on the counter and his head resting in his hands.

Marian placed a hand on his shoulder. "We'll find them. I know we will," she said in a forced certainty that even she didn't believe.

When Joe raised his head to face her, she saw the exhaustion that lined his face. "Oh, really? And how might we do that? The entire town is in a state of emergency, and ice has been coming down for hours. It's treacherous out there, and there's no way I can go out looking for them without the risk of leaving my daughter fatherless."

The frustration in Joe's voice caused Marian to remove her hand and take a step back. "I don't know how, but I know you'll get to the bottom of this theft. You're a very capable sheriff. I know you'll do what needs to be done."

Rubbing his hand over the stubble on his face, he muttered, "What is it with Christmas in this town? This is the third year in a row that we've had some kind of crime. I miss the days when *nothing* exciting ever happened around here."

"Most of the time it's quiet," Eli reminded him. "We can be grateful for that." Eli stood, leaning against the counter with Holly pulled close him, her back to his chest.

"That's true, Joe," Holly agreed. "It stinks that Christmas is the time of year when we seem to have a crime spree, but most of the time this is a quiet little place to live. For everyone that wasn't here tonight, it still is a quiet place to live."

Joe harrumphed and stood from his seat. "There's nothing we can do tonight. Let's all get a little shuteye and start fresh tomorrow."

Eli, Holly, and Marian nodded in agreement. It had been a long evening and staying up later wouldn't help find Louise Hubley's missing jewelry.

Marian snapped off the lights as the others bundled up to walk out into the frozen wonderland Saddle Hill had become during the past few hours.

"I'm going to stop in and tell Nadine goodnight and hopefully get to see Josie before I head over," Marian heard Joe tell Eli.

She shook her head. What a night this was turning out to be. First, the ice storm had come out of nowhere, leaving them all stranded, then a couple of thieves made off with jewelry they'd swiped from another guest.

As she flipped the final switch, the kitchen—the coziest part of the house—was plunged into darkness. Walking through the door, she crunched her way across the field, lagging behind the others. A glance over her shoulder at her beloved restored farmhouse revealed that the lights in all the bedroom windows were off except the one with views of the garden—the one the Hubleys were staying in.

With a sigh, Marian wondered how much damage would be done to her reputation and the future of the bed-and-breakfast once word got out that it had been the scene of another crime.

Chapter Nineteen

"CAN YOU BELIEVE Holly refused to come with us?" Sylvia asked Nadine as she pulled the covers back on one of the twin-sized beds in one of Marian's guest rooms.

Nadine shrugged in response as she tucked her baby daughter into a bassinet next to her bed. "I suppose I can. Marriage has softened her."

Sylvia snorted. "Softened? You call that stubborn streak 'soft'?"

Nadine chuckled. "She wants to help Eli. She'd do anything for him. If she thinks she's helping him by sticking around the farmhouse and being a pain in the neck to us and everyone around her, then yes, I'd call her stubborn streak 'soft,'" Nadine said before turning her attention back to Josephine.

Sliding between the covers, Sylvia fluffed the pillow and rested her head on it. "Whatever you say." She turned her head toward Nadine and asked, "Do you ever think I'll have what you have? What Holly has?"

Confident that Josephine was content, Nadine slid into her own bed and turned her attention to Sylvia. "What we have? The patience of a saint because these guys never put the seat down?"

Sylvia laughed dryly. "Oh, you know. A 'happily ever after.'"

"I'm sure you've got men banging the door down to get to you. If you stopped working so much and made time to have a personal life, I'm sure you'd find your 'happily ever after,' as you called it. In fact, I think I know one of the men who would gladly volunteer to help with that."

Nadine's sly smile caused a rush of heat to wash up Sylvia's neck and onto her cheeks, but she didn't respond.

Nadine arched an eyebrow. "Looks to me like you know who I'm talking about, and that he might not be the only one who's interested," she commented, sliding farther under her covers and pulling the blanket up to her chin.

The wind howled against the windows, reminding the women how lucky they were to have a friend to take them in when they couldn't make it to their own homes.

After listening to the ice rapping against the window for a few minutes, Sylvia finally said in a quiet voice, "We're so different. It would never work."

Nadine couldn't help but notice the disappointment in her friend's words. "Your differences will only get in the way if you let them. Sometimes we have to look past what someone is on the outside to see the goodness inside." Glancing at Sylvia, who was now chewing her bottom lip, she added, "Just look at Joe. You know how grumpy he can be. When I first met him I had to work really hard to ignore the permanent scowl on his face, and even though it's not there as often, sometimes I still have to force myself to look past it. I see the good in him. He's a wonderful husband and father, and even though he doesn't always show it, he cares deeply for his friends and family. He'd do anything for all of us."

"I guess so…" Sylvia agreed.

"Just think about it," Nadine suggested as she reached for the lamp on the bedside table and switched off the light. "You'll never know unless you give it a shot."

A deep sigh was Sylvia's only response.

Lying in the dark and staring toward the ceiling, Nadine hoped that she'd gotten through to her glamorous friend. Life was so very short, and she hated to see Sylvia lonely. She had a hunch that her friend was rethinking some of the choices she'd made, and that she was on the verge of making some life-changing decisions. Nadine could only hope that Sylvia could put aside her pride and take a chance on a man who thought she hung the moon.

Chapter Twenty

KRIS JINGLE SAT sprawled in the overstuffed armchair next to the fireplace in Vito's half of the duplex. Since he was stuck here for an undetermined amount of time, he figured he might as well study for his finals that were coming up next week—assuming they weren't still stuck here by then.

Vito eyed him curiously as Kris furiously jotted notes in the margins of the book he was reading.

"Must be interesting," Vito observed.

Kris raised his eyes from the biography of Shakespeare and nodded. "Technically, this course was an elective, but if I plan to teach English literature someday, *The Life and Times of William Shakespeare* should have been a requirement."

"Shakespeare, huh? I have to admit I don't know much about him other than he wrote *Romeo and Juliet* and a bunch of other famous plays," Vito continued.

"That's not surprising," Kris quipped.

Vito arched an eyebrow at his roommate for the night.

Noticing how that must have come across, Kris stammered, "I mean, most people don't know a lot about Shakespeare, and *Romeo and Juliet* is one of his most famous works. Everyone has heard of that one."

A smirk tugged at the corner of Vito's mouth. "I knew what you meant."

Silence floated between the two men for a long minute before Kris spoke. "How's it been going for you since last Christmas?"

Vito's mouth dipped into a frown. "Since I kidnapped Marian and was arrested, you mean?"

Kris could feel the heat creeping up his neck, over his cheeks, and toward his receding hairline. "Sure, if that's how you want to mark your time. I know it's probably been rough for you. Marian is the town's most beloved citizen. I'm sure our other residents didn't take too kindly to you kidnapping her."

Trying to sit taller, Vito pulled his shoulders back and straightened his spine. "Marian has been great. She's the most forgiving person I've ever met. Once everybody saw that she's okay with me, others accepted me as well. I'm hoping that in time people will forget what I did and see me for who I am."

Kris placed his pen inside his book to mark his page, closed it, and set it on the small table beside the chair. "They will. It takes a little while for people to forget the jail part, but eventually they move on."

Rubbing his chin, Vito leaned slightly forward in Kris's direction. "Sounds like you have personal experience."

A rueful smile tugged at Kris's mouth. "Yeah. Unfortunately, I do. I was a guest of the Saddle Hill jail for a short time Christmas before last."

"You're kidding!" Vito's eyebrows shot toward his hairline.

"Mr. English Lit was a resident of the Saddle Hill jail? I wasn't expecting that."

"I wish I was kidding. It was awful." Kris shuddered. "Fortunately, I didn't have to stay very long. I was arrested for stealing a special Christmas piece from Stockton's Jewel Palace, but Marian and Joe finally proved that I was framed." He snorted. "By my own brother, of all people."

Vito shook his head. "That's terrible," he muttered. "Your brother?"

Kris nodded and launched into his family history—the year-round Christmas, the obsession with Santa Claus, and how he was always the black sheep of the very merry Jingle family. Ending with his mom's memoir about living in an eternal Christmas, Kris wrapped up his story to his captive audience.

"Hard to believe that was two years ago," Kris muttered.

"Wow," Vito breathed. "That's wild. At least you were innocent, though. I was guilty as sin, but Marian took pity on me and got me out of jail and gave me a job here. She's really something," Vito added, almost to himself.

"Yeah, well, I dated the woman that hired to you to kidnap Marian. I sure know how to pick 'em. No wonder I've never been married," Kris said mournfully.

Vito's eyes widened. "You dated that Carol Ling person? Man, she was ruthless. She tried to kill me and wanted to let Marian starve to death. A cold, cold lady, that one."

Kris nodded sadly. "Like I said, I know how to pick 'em." In his mid-thirties, Kris was one of the only single guys his age in town. It was his relationship with Carol that had awoken the desire to share his life with someone else. Unfortunately, the pickings were slim and the one he'd thought was *the one* was now sitting behind bars.

"How about you? Ever been married?" Kris queried.

Vito grunted. "Yeah, for a few years. I've got two kids I never get to see."

Kris dropped his eyes to his book. "I'm sorry." Though he'd never really liked kids, especially in his role as Santa listening to their endless Christmas lists, he imagined it must be pretty painful not being able to see your own.

Shrugging a shoulder, Vito said, "I'm used to it. My wife took off with some big-city lawyer type and never looked back. They've got money, I don't. I've gotten myself in trouble with last year's kidnapping. There's no reason a judge would order her to let me see them. He'd find her claim that I'm not a suitable father credible."

Kris raised his eyes to look at the man sitting near him, brooding over his lost family. A stab of compassion overwhelmed him. "If there's anything I can do, let me know. I can be a character witness or whatever they call the people who speak up for you in court."

One side of Vito's drooping mouth twitched. "Thanks, man. Nobody has ever offered that before."

"Nobody? Ever?" Kris asked incredulously. "No friends helped?"

"Somehow I managed to lose my friends along the way. There was nobody left to speak up for me."

Kris shook his head in disbelief. He'd always thought he had it bad, but when he got into trouble, he at least had people who were there for him, trying to find the truth when he couldn't do it himself. It must have been terrible for Vito to not have that. "Well, there are people here now," Kris assured him.

The flames continued to lick the logs when the moment between the two men was interrupted. James Jingle stomped in, nose red from the cold and ice lingering in his hair.

Vito sat up straighter. "Do you know if they've had any luck finding out who robbed the Hubleys?"

James's mouth formed a grim line and shook his head. "Not that I've heard, but I doubt there's much they can do tonight. Where can I clean up?"

Rising from his chair, Vito led James down the hallway to a bathroom. Kris listened to him instructing his father on where he should sleep, and decided right then that Vito was a nice guy who needed his help.

Chapter Twenty-One

THE ICE THAT coated the grounds of the Farmhouse Inn Bed & Breakfast shimmered in the morning light. Marian, wrapped in her fleece robe, held a cup of coffee to her lips and looked out the frost-framed window. On a different morning, the idyllic scene would have filled Marian with a sense of well-being.

"Beautiful, isn't it?" Sylvia said from behind her.

Marian turned toward her friend. "It is," she agreed. "Did you sleep okay?"

Sylvia, dressed in the clothes she wore the day before, nodded. "Pretty well, considering."

"I'm sorry I didn't have anything for you to wear to bed," Marian apologized, then nodded toward her slightly rumpled sweater and velvet pants. "I'm just a tad shorter than you."

Sylvia smiled and shrugged. "And by a 'tad shorter' you mean a solid eight inches. I guess none of us expected this," she said, waving toward the window at the ice-covered grass. "Otherwise we would have come prepared."

"Unfortunately, a lot of things have happened that we didn't expect," the older woman said thoughtfully.

Sylvia chewed on her lower lip. "I'm so sorry it's ended up like this. To think that your guests have been robbed! I can't even imagine what that must feel like. For them or you."

Taking another sip of her coffee, Marian then patted Sylvia's forearm. "It will be okay. I didn't get to this age by seeing the worst in everything. I just wish there was something I could do…"

Sylvia draped an arm around Marian's shoulders. "Just be you. That's more than enough. I doubt any of the guests would even dream of blaming you personally for what's happened. Unfortunately, there are just people out there who make their selfishness everyone else's problem."

Bobbing her head in agreement, Marian drained the last of the coffee from her mug. "I better get ready to head back to the farmhouse. I've got a lot of people to feed today."

Releasing the motherly woman, Sylvia said, "I'll help. I've got to earn my keep, and I'm sure everybody else feels the same way."

"I would appreciate that, thank you," Marian said, then turned to walk back toward her bedroom, her brow furrowed in thought.

What could she possibly do to help her guests feel glad to be there? She acknowledged that it's one thing to go somewhere remote and *choose* to stay cooped up there, but that it's a different thing altogether to be *forced* to stay in a place that's both isolated and unfamiliar.

"The Christmas season should be one of joy and wonder," Marian muttered to herself as she opened the door of her closet.

"Feeling trapped this time of year is the last thing a person needs."

As she looked through her vast selection of Christmas sweaters, she vowed that she would bring the spirit of Christmas to her guests, even if she was surrounded by a bunch of Scrooges.

Selecting her outfit for the day, her mouth turned upward into a mischievous grin. As she hummed "Jingle Bells," she began planning a day full of festivities to get the guests in a holiday mood.

She spun in front of her closet mirror and sang out, *"Jingle all the waaaaaay!"*

If this didn't help take their minds off the circumstances they all found themselves in, nothing would.

Chapter Twenty-Two

MARIAN BUSTLED AROUND the kitchen with Ivy Wood by her side. "We need to do the best we can to make a hearty breakfast for everyone," Marian instructed as she gathered the ingredients for her grandmother's beloved buttermilk biscuits.

"Yes, ma'am," Ivy said, obediently. "What's on the menu?"

A smile curved Marian's lips. "Biscuits and gravy, roasted figs with cranberries and cinnamon, bacon, eggs, and orange juice."

Ivy's eyes widened. "That's a lot of food. Are you sure we have enough for all that? I mean, we still don't know exactly how long we'll all be here and when we'll be able to get more food. We don't want to run out."

Marian nodded in agreement. "Exactly. If we feed them a giant breakfast, then have some snacks in the afternoon, they won't be hungry for lunch. I have some activities planned for today as long as I can get everyone on board."

"You're the boss. We'll do whatever you think is best," Ivy conceded.

Giving her newest employee an affirmative nod, Marian and Ivy got to work crafting the morning feast for their guests.

A gust of wind preceded the entry of Sylvia, Holly, and Nadine by mere seconds. "Good morning," the trio sang out cheerily as they waltzed into the kitchen.

"Good morning, girls!" Marian chirped as she walked over to greet each one with a hug and a kiss on the cheek. "How did everyone sleep?"

"Like a log," Nadine said, bouncing baby Josephine on her hip. "This one finally decided to sleep through the night. I think she liked having her favorite aunts and Grandma Marian around. Either that or she was exhausted from all the attention she got."

"Wonderful!" Marian exclaimed, tickling the little girl's chubby knee.

"I didn't sleep great. I was up too late and have a lot on my mind," Holly said. "I'm hoping we can be of some help today and that Eli and Joe can figure out who took Mrs. Hubley's jewelry. Then we can just enjoy our time here together."

"Same," Sylvia echoed. "It's too bad I don't have any concealer to hide the circles under my eyes. I'm dangerously close to looking my age," she added with a wink in Marian's direction.

"Oh, pish posh. You're beautiful and everybody knows it," Marian said with a mischievous smile.

Sylvia dropped her eyes to the toes of her winter boots while Nadine, Holly, and Marian shared a knowing glance.

"Nadine, I'll go with you to get Josephine settled and run through a list of things I have planned for today. They will be absolutely impossible without your help," the older lady confessed.

"Yes, ma'am," Nadine replied as she left the kitchen with Marian at her heels.

"I'm going to go check on Eli and see if they need me for anything," Holly said, then disappeared through the door leading to the dining room.

Sylvia grabbed a spare apron from a hook near the double oven and slipped it over her head. As she tied the strings behind her, she faced Ivy. "What can I do to help?"

After rattling off a list of things that needed to be done, Ivy turned back to her task of cracking eggs.

Soon, Sylvia was whisking milk into the flour-and-sausage-grease mixture, careful to make sure no lumps remained in the gravy. "I don't see how people can eat like this every day. If I did, I'd be as big as a house. Or maybe I'd have dropped dead of a heart attack before I had the chance to gain that much weight."

"A lot of people do, unfortunately," Ivy replied, her words laced with sadness. "My dad did, anyway."

"I'm so sorry," Sylvia said with compassion.

"It's not your fault," Ivy said. "I learned from his mistakes, though. I won't touch this stuff now." She waved her hand around the kitchen. "No meat, eggs, or butter for me."

Managing to mask her surprise, she returned to the task of making the gravy. She never would have guessed she'd find a vegetarian here. If she lived in Saddle Hill full-time, it would be a lot harder to eat a balanced diet. With the way things were now, though, the occasional indulgence didn't do much harm.

"I need to go set the table for breakfast," Ivy announced. "When you're finished with the gravy, will you start on the biscuits? Marian is very particular about them, and I just don't have the guts to try." With a weak smile, Ivy was gone.

Sylvia set to work sifting the flour, cutting the shortening into the dry mixture, and measuring the buttermilk, pausing at every step to consult the recipe.

A deep chuckle behind her caused her to pause and turn toward the direction of the door leading outside. Vito stood there, a load of firewood in his arms, eyes fixed on Sylvia.

"You have flour on your face," he said, eyes dancing with a mixture of amusement and tenderness.

She swiped at her cheek, but the effort was met with more laughter. "You made it worse," Vito pointed out. "Let me take this wood to the fireplace and I'll be back to help you."

When Vito walked out of the kitchen, Sylvia allowed herself to heave a sigh of relief. She couldn't remember ever feeling like she'd been tied up in knots around a man before. Yes, they were very different, and yes, he had kidnapped one of her dearest friends last year, but there was something about him. Something about the way he cared about his work and the people around him that was a breath of fresh air compared to so many of the people she knew who were only concerned about a paycheck.

Conscious of the fact that it would only take a minute or two to unload the firewood he'd been carrying, Sylvia dusted off her hands over the sink and brushed as much of the flour off her face as she could without a mirror.

Forcing herself to focus, she once again skimmed over the recipe for the biscuits, finished mixing the dough, and, after patting it out on the counter, began cutting the biscuits.

A quick glance at the clock on the wall revealed that

breakfast would be served in half an hour. Working as quickly as she could, Sylvia placed the biscuits on the tray, then popped the tray into the oven.

Ivy hadn't come back yet—and neither had Vito—so Sylvia grabbed a clean whisk, the shredded cheese, heavy cream, and salt and pepper and got the eggs ready to scramble. She hadn't expected to be doing so much of the work for breakfast, but by the time Ivy came back to the kitchen, the only thing left to do was fry the bacon.

When Marian rang the bell giving the guests a ten-minute warning that breakfast was about to be served, Sylvia plopped on a stool at the counter and exhaled.

It had already been a busy morning, and the day was just getting started.

Chapter Twenty-Three

VITO LOWERED THE stack of firewood he carried into the log holder by the fireplace, removed a few pieces to arrange in the firebox and stood back up. The sight of Sylvia in the kitchen wearing an apron and socks on her feet had been a jolt he wasn't expecting. This morning, slightly rumpled and doing such a normal task as cooking breakfast, she looked like a regular woman—a woman who might be found in the kitchen of any home—and less like the out-of-reach fashion icon she really was.

He exhaled sharply. It was cruel, really. When he saw her he'd allowed himself a brief moment of dreaming. What would it be like to have her in his kitchen making breakfast for him? With the flour streaked across her cheek she'd looked adorable. The girl next door.

Except she wasn't the girl next door. She wasn't even the girl next town over. She was the girl out of reach.

Angry with himself for even entertaining the notion that she'd ever look at him the way he wanted her to, he stooped over the fireplace, wadded a piece of newspaper and lit it with a match he pulled from his pocket. Stuffing the burning paper between the logs, he waited while they caught fire and stood up.

He heard the breakfast bell, alerting everyone that breakfast would be in about ten minutes.

He brushed off the hearth, removing any wooden splinters or bark that might have chipped away from the wood. With a final glance, he was satisfied that no trace of his work had been left behind.

Vito forced himself to smile. He liked his work, and he enjoyed making the Farmhouse Inn a nice place to stay. He loved Marian like a mother and wanted to help her succeed more than almost anything. He'd been content this last year, and he knew it was silly to give that up for a woman, no matter how beautiful she was.

With a renewed determination, Vito left the dining room, the fire ablaze, and walked out of the house through the front door.

Especially now that there was ice on everything, there was work to be done.

Chapter Twenty-Four

"MY, MY. YOU girls have gotten a lot done!" Marian remarked when she finally came back to the kitchen.

Ivy pushed her chin-length blond hair behind her ear and said, "This was mostly Sylvia. Who knew that when she was given a task, she'd take to it like a woman possessed?"

"It was fun," Sylvia said with a shrug. Besides, she thought, it gave me something to occupy my mind that had nothing to do with Vito.

"Well, if it tastes as good as it looks and smells, you might have a job offer coming your way, dear." Marian winked and laughed softly at her own joke. "Let's get these platters out there."

Marian, Sylvia, and Ivy gathered the different trays of food and carried them out to the waiting crowd.

Several of the guests had already taken their seats, though Cassandra Weaver was noticeably absent.

"Maybe she won't come," Marian said under her breath in a voice loud enough for only Sylvia to hear.

Sylvia, too, had gotten a strange feeling about Cassandra. She wasn't much of a conversationalist and wouldn't have seemed any more isolated if she'd been the only one in the room. Nadine had said something about her being a "cat lady." For whatever reason, that usually meant a person was a loner. Although, why would somebody want to come to a bed-and-breakfast on their own, then avoid everyone else there? It just seemed sad. No significant other, no girlfriend getaway. Just aloneness. Sylvia shook her head. A person could be alone anywhere.

"Sylvia, dear, you can put the tray down," Marian said gently.

"Oh, of course." Sylvia hadn't even realized she was still holding the tray with the platter of biscuits and the bowl of gravy on it. Now that she was aware, the load began to feel heavy. She put the tray on the buffet, then unloaded its contents onto the dining table.

Food made with love now covered the table and a fire roared in the fireplace, bringing with it the feeling that all was right in the world. Despite the cold and dangerous weather conditions, right now in this house, there was joy and warmth. Even though there had been a theft last night, the morning carried the potential for goodness.

It was the most wonderful time of the year, and glancing at the faces around her, Sylvia was certain that they were all determined to enjoy this day to its absolute fullest.

Chapter Twenty-Five

WITH A CROWD gathered at the table around the breakfast Sylvia and Ivy had prepared, and a fire blazing in the fireplace, thanks to Vito, everything felt right with the world—at least for the moment. Friends laughed together and brought the Hubleys into their circle, trying their best to help them forget about the fact that they had been robbed the night before.

The only person still on the premises who wasn't at breakfast was Cassandra Weaver.

Grant Hubley, with dark circles under his eyes, took a sip of his coffee. Louise didn't look much more alert, though she tried to make pleasant conversation.

"Looks like we've got some sleepyheads," she observed, taking notice of the empty chairs at the table.

"Guess so," Marian murmured while she refilled Professor Hubley's coffee cup. "It's a good morning to sleep in. I'm just thankful we still have electricity. It's not uncommon for these storms to knock the power out. It happens just about every winter."

"Young people tend to value sleep more than food," Grant said, ignoring Marian's comment about the electricity. "I suppose the Turner folks are still snoozing away. And though she's no spring chicken, Ms. Weaver is still young enough to sleep well."

Joe and Marian shared a quick look. At the flash of panic in Marian's eyes, Joe cleared his throat. "It does appear that Ms. Weaver isn't much of a breakfast eater."

"Doesn't look like it," Eli said, then cheerfully added, "I'll be more than happy to eat her share of breakfast. This is delicious."

Several of the others nodded in agreement as they shoveled food into their mouths and chewed.

"I'm afraid I can't take credit for breakfast this morning," Marian confessed. "Sylvia and Ivy were kind enough to take care of it so I could focus my efforts elsewhere."

"I didn't know you were such a good cook, Sylvia," Nadine said with a smile. "Maybe we should throw a dinner party sometime. You take care of the main course and I'll make dessert."

"Sounds like fun," Sylvia replied, acutely aware that Vito was studying her from his seat at the table.

"That's a great idea!" Holly said enthusiastically. "I'm still not much of a cook, but I'll be happy to pitch in wherever I can."

"I've never had fruit roasted like this," Kris chimed in. "Mom, how come you never roasted fruit?"

"Never thought of it," Patricia answered with a shrug, then focused on her own pile of fruit. "You're right, though. It is good."

Sylvia tilted her head toward Ivy and said, "Ivy roasted the fruit."

Kris shot an appreciative glance toward the young blond woman. "It's delicious."

Tucking a stray strand of hair behind her ear, Ivy said a shy "Thank you."

They held one another's gaze for several seconds before Holly interrupted the moment. "Did everyone sleep okay? Marian, your house is so cozy."

"We slept alright, considering…" Mr. Hubley offered. "It's hard to relax completely when there's a thief roaming around."

"I slept like a log," James Jingle said. "I admit I was worried about sleeping on an air mattress, but young Vito here gave me his bed and took the air mattress instead. I've got no stiff joints or anything this morning. Well, no more than I usually do, that is."

Sylvia cast a glance toward Vito, who, when he noticed she was watching him, looked down at his plate and swirled his fork through his gravy.

"That was very kind of you," she murmured.

"It sure saved my back," James piped in. "I doubt I'd even be able to walk today if I'd slept on that air mattress."

"Nobody wants that," Marian affirmed as she walked around with the coffee pot, refilling the cups. She stopped when she reached Louise Hubley and placed her free hand on the woman's back. "And how are you doing, dear? I know things were tough last evening."

Tears glistened in Louise's eyes. "I just can't believe I've lost something that was so special to me."

Grant let his coffee cup land heavily in its saucer. "Come

now, Louise. Nothing that was taken was particularly valuable. It can be replaced."

The professor's wife narrowed her eyes at him. "Well, to me those things were *very* valuable. Just because you lack sentiment, doesn't mean those items were unimportant."

Awkward silence filled the dining room as everyone except the Hubleys focused on their plates. Louise still glared at her husband.

Breaking the silence, Vito cleared his throat and scooted his chair back. "I think I'll go check on the weather and road conditions and see if there's any update on how long the mayor is advising people to stay put. It might not be a bad idea to make sure the generator is in working order, either."

"Good idea," Marian agreed. "Please be sure to let us know what you find out."

A single nod of his head was Vito's only response as he left the room.

"Well," Marian breathed, "with any luck Vito will find out that things weren't as bad as expected, and let's keep our fingers crossed that we won't need that generator."

As the group finished the meal, Nadine and Ivy began clearing the dishes and serving platters from the table. With so many people being stuck here, they needed to get started on snacks and preparing the next meal.

It was clear by the expression on each face that they all agreed Marian's statement had been nothing more than wishful thinking. They'd all heard the ice pelting the windows and roof, and everyone could see that ice covered everything outside as far as the eye could see.

Though it was beautiful, everyone knew danger awaited if anyone tried to leave the safety of the farmhouse.

The last of the dishes finally cleared, the group disbanded. Just as everyone was about to leave the dining room, a breathless Cassandra Weaver came darting into the room.

Her face flushed and eyes wide, she shrieked, "I've been robbed!"

The crowd exchanged worried glances with one another. Then there was a loud *POP!* and the lights went out.

Chapter Twenty-Six

GASPS COULD BE heard throughout the dim room that was now lit only by the windows and gloomy sky outside.

"Robbed?" someone murmured.

"How could that be?" asked someone else.

"Quiet down, everybody. Marian, you might want to find Vito and tell him we need that generator up and running ASAP," Joe commanded. Stepping forward toward the trembling woman, he said, "Tell me what happened."

Ms. Weaver swallowed hard. "I had a diamond chain. It's gone!" she wailed, her face buried in her hands.

"When was the last time you saw it?" the sheriff queried.

Cassandra wrapped her arms around herself. "It's so cold in here."

"Let's go to the sitting room where you can sit closer to the fire," Joe suggested. "Nadine, will you please get Ms. Weaver some coffee?" *Decaf,* he mouthed as he led the newest robbery victim from the room.

"Another one?" Professor Hubley asked, exasperated. "What kind of place is this?" he shot at Marian.

"Grant," Louise scolded, "this isn't her fault. Don't act like that."

"How am I supposed to act? I've just retired and was looking for some peace and quiet. I find this hole-in-the-wall bed-and-breakfast that promises to be a serene escape from the hustle and bustle of everyday life, and we get robbed! Now someone else is in the exact same position." He turned toward the group of Saddle Hill locals. "Which one of you did it? If nobody can leave and nobody can get here, that just leaves one of you," Grant growled, pointing an accusatory finger at the group.

"You wait right there," Eli said, stepping forward. "Don't start accusing people you don't know anything about. These people are some of the best folks I've ever known, and I won't have you calling any one of them thieves."

Louise placed a hand on her husband's arm. "Grant, honey, I think we'd better go to our room so you can settle down. Shouting at people isn't going to help the situation."

Though grumbling, he allowed his wife to take him back to their room.

"Far cry from the jovial fella we met yesterday," James Jingle announced once the couple was out of earshot. "To think any of this is Marian's fault is ludicrous."

"I don't think he was blaming her, per se," Sylvia interjected, "but you can understand why he'd feel sour about their experience here so far. He was robbed, now Cassandra Weaver." She shook her head. "And here we thought the Turners were somehow involved in the theft. If they're long gone, though, I guess it can't be them."

"Let's wait and hear what Joe learns before we jump to any conclusions. Maybe she forgot to bring her diamond chain with her, or maybe it was already gone and she just now noticed it." Eli shrugged as he spoke. "Right now we have more questions than answers."

"Who would bring diamonds to stay at a farmhouse?" Kris wondered aloud. "That just seems ridiculous."

"It takes all kinds," Patricia murmured. "Maybe she hoped to meet someone here."

Kris shrugged. "She'd have to be a little more sociable than this."

No one else spoke, but several nodded in agreement. Cassandra Weaver didn't seem the type to pick up a guy on vacation.

A hum filled the silence moments before the lights flickered back on.

"Looks like Vito got the generator working," Marian announced, relief evident in her voice as she turned to Nadine. "I'll go find out what he learned about the road conditions. You and Ivy can go ahead and start preparations for our first activity."

As Marian left the room, Nadine's glance toward Ivy communicated what they were all thinking: the guests weren't going to care a bit about learning to decorate Christmas cookies when there was a thief on the loose.

Chapter Twenty-Seven

"TAKE ME THROUGH this again," Joe said, matching the impatience he was getting from Cassandra Weaver.

She huffed. "I've already told you what happened. Didn't you listen the first time?"

Through gritted teeth, Joe growled, "That's why I said 'again.' Take me through it *again*. If I'm going to help you, I need you to drop the attitude and make sure I have all the information I need and that I understand what you've tried to communicate. If you want me to help you find your diamonds, you've got to work with me."

Crossing her arms over her chest, Cassandra huffed. "Fine. I have a diamond chain that was in a zipped outer pocket of my suitcase. It's not there anymore, so obviously somebody stole it. That Bright woman has some nerve letting criminals stay here."

"Marian has no control over what kind of people check in. It's not customary to run background checks on guests. Now, this is a pretty out-of-the-way place, and it says so on the website where you likely booked your stay. Would you mind telling me what you needed diamonds for at a place like this?"

Cassandra glared at him. "As a matter a fact, I *do* mind, but I'll tell you anyway since I'm feeling generous. Sometimes a lady wants to have beautiful jewelry with her."

She fancies herself a *lady*? Joe thought with a mixture of humor and disbelief. This is the grouchiest woman I've ever come across.

"Have you worn it or had it out of your bag since you arrived yesterday?"

"No, I have not."

"Do you suppose it could be anywhere in your suite? Maybe it fell out somehow."

Casting a glance at Joe that communicated just how stupid she thought he was, Ms. Weaver ground out, "Impossible. I haven't even unzipped that pocket."

Joe nodded. This woman was impossible, not the notion that it could have fallen out of the pocket. Instead of voicing his thoughts, he said, "Would you mind if Deputy Nolan and I did a thorough search of your room in an effort to find the jewelry?"

"As a matter of fact, I *would* mind, Sheriff. It's not very gentlemanly for you to go digging through a lady's belongings."

There's that lady bit again, Joe thought, using all his effort to keep from rolling his eyes. "Well ma'am, if you didn't want me to help you, can you tell me why you came to me shouting about a robbery in the first place?"

Indignant, Cassandra said, "So you know what kind of place this is! I've been to a lot of places in my life, but this is the first time I've ever been the victim of theft. Think about that, Sheriff. The 'wonderful' little town you all rave about is a hotbed for crime. I read the news accounts about the stuff that's been going on here the last two years. In my opinion, it's time for Saddle Hill to look for another sheriff."

Joe flushed hot at the woman's biting remark. She wasn't even a local with voting rights, so who was she to have an opinion on the matter? Leave it to someone as negative as her to completely gloss over the fact that he'd arrested the criminal last year, and assisted in the arrest of one the year before he was ever even sheriff. Never mind the fact that he'd received an award for his efforts last year by the mayor herself. He bit his lip to keep from saying the things that were swirling through his head.

At the metallic taste of blood, he growled. "Well, you know where to find me if you want help finding your diamonds." With that he spun on his heel and stomped off to the kitchen, muttering under his breath the whole way. He couldn't decide which he was angrier about: Cassandra Weaver's attitude or the fact that there had now been two thefts right under his nose; never mind his gut feeling that there was something very, very off about the latest robbery victim.

Chapter Twenty-Eight

"DID YOU FIND out anything?" Eli asked when Joe entered the kitchen.

Despite the activity in there during breakfast preparations, the room was spotless. The counters and white cabinets shone with a warm glow under the pendant lights hanging overhead.

Joe ignored the question for a moment and went straight for the coffee maker. After pouring himself a large mug full of the special winter blend that was Marian's year-round favorite, he turned toward his deputy and took a gulp of the steaming liquid. He swallowed, then grunted, "Yeah. I learned that woman is a complete kook."

"Do you want some creamer?" Marian asked, extending the bottle of eggnog-flavored creamer she preferred during the Christmas season. It was obvious to Joe that Marian bustled around the kitchen as a way to keep herself busy, most likely as a distraction from the mess her guests were in.

"Thanks, but I'll pass," Joe said, taking another big drink. "This is good stuff," he said absently.

Marian bobbed her head in response but stayed quiet.

"So, what happened?" Eli asked, his arm draped loosely around Holly's shoulder.

The whole Saddle Hill crew was gathered in the kitchen, Ralph and Carla seated with James and Patricia on stools at the island, Sylvia and Nadine leaning against the counter. Kris nibbled a leftover biscuit while also keeping an eye on Ivy, who leaned over the counter as she made a list across the counter from the Stocktons and the elder Jingles. Vito stood off in a corner by himself, visibly at a loss about how to occupy himself.

Each one had their eyes fixed on Joe, waiting to hear what happened with Cassandra Weaver.

Joe cleared his throat. "Well, she said she brought the jewelry with her, even though the Farmhouse Inn is in a pretty remote spot, because sometimes a 'lady' wants to have beautiful jewelry with her." He rolled his eyes for emphasis. "She swears she didn't take the diamond chain out of her bag, though she had it stashed in an outside zipper compartment. In my opinion, it probably fell out."

"A hole in the pocket, maybe?" Sylvia suggested.

Shrugging, Joe drained his coffee cup, set it on the counter with a thump and faced the fashion icon. "She says it's not possible. Though, I have no proof of that," he added. "She won't let me look."

Narrowing his eyes, Eli dropped his arm to his side from Holly's shoulders and, with his brows knitted in a frown, said, "What do you mean you have no proof? Shouldn't her word be enough? I mean, she would have checked her bag, don't you think?"

"It would only be that simple in a perfect world," Joe groused. "She refused to let me check anything out. She said it wouldn't be very gentlemanly of me to go through her things. Apparently a lady needs her privacy," Joe said in a mocking tone, one that all his friends knew was his feeble attempt to mask his frustration. "She is by far the least cooperative victim I've ever met. It's almost like she doesn't want help."

"What do we do then?" Eli snapped incredulously. "We've got—or at least had—a robber staying here, and our hands are tied? That's ridiculous! We must be able to do *something* to investigate," the young deputy said. Though his voice was frustrated, his face held a helpless look. "Why won't she cooperate? I mean, she was definitely weird when I tried to search her room after Mrs. Hubley's stuff went missing. What's that lady's problem?"

Joe shrugged and grabbed the coffee pot for a refill.

"Maybe she's acting like this because there was never any robbery. Of her stuff, I mean," Kris suggested. "It's possible she made the story up and you wouldn't find her diamond chain because there never was one."

Chewing on his lip, Joe considered the possibility. "You may have a point there," he admitted.

"Or maybe she's the thief and she faked a robbery to throw suspicion off herself," Sylvia theorized.

"Both are good possibilities," Eli said. "Joe, call the judge at home and ask him for a warrant to search the guests' rooms. We won't need one for the Turners' room since they already split, but we'd still need one for the Hubleys' and the Weaver woman's."

The sheriff nodded his head in agreement. "I'd hoped everyone would cooperate and it wouldn't come to this, but it looks like it has." He pulled his cell phone from his belt. As he pulled up the judge's number, he asked, "Marian, can I use your office to make the call? I don't want the guests to overhear."

"Of course," Marian replied, her attempt at lightheartedness falling flat. When Joe was in her office, the door closed behind him, Marian turned toward the others. "Now, I'll need everyone to vacate my kitchen. We've got things to do. This won't be just a dreary winter day on my watch." Her eyes twinkled as everyone except Nadine, Ivy, and herself walked toward the sitting room.

"I've got the list all ready," Ivy offered, and the three women huddled together to go over the list and prepare for the day's upcoming festivities.

Even though there was a thief on the loose, the Turners had flown the coop, and the guests who were left were melancholy at best, Marian was determined to provide opportunities for everyone to be wrapped in the warm glow of the season all day long.

Chapter Twenty-Nine

T HE JINGLES, STOCKTONS, Holly, Sylvia, and Vito sat around the fire still roaring in the fireplace in the sitting room.

"What a twist of events, huh?" Carla murmured, her gaze fixed on the flames in front of her.

"No kidding," Sylvia concurred. "I hate that Marian's first Christmas here is turning out like this."

Several heads nodded in agreement.

"It just seems like she can't get a break these last few Christmases," Ralph said, gazing steadily at the flames licking the logs in the fireplace. "All since Roger died, too."

"I'm certainly to blame for some of that," Vito admitted, looking down at his callused hands. "I'm responsible for what was probably the worst Christmas of her life." A soft, ironic chuckle escaped from his throat. "And yet she did her best to make sure I was doing okay and kept me well-fed while I held her hostage."

Sylvia shifted her dark brown eyes to Vito. Her gaze

softened, compassion spilling from it. "She loves you, Vito, and she forgave you a long time ago. I'm sure Marian considers you one of her closest friends now. Like it or not, you're part of the group, no matter what you did in the past. I think we can all agree that Saddle Hill is a great place for new beginnings."

Holly reached over and clasped Sylvia's hand. "That's certainly been the case for me. Before I came here, I'd been arrested for shoplifting and done time in jail. My life turned around, all because Marian saw something in me that no one else did and welcomed me into her home. Now look where I am. I have a husband—in law enforcement, ironically—and better friends than I'd ever had in my life. Friends who care about me and each other, and constantly go out of their way to help one another. You're part of that now, Vito," Holly assured him.

Vito blinked rapidly, leaving the others to wonder if he was tearing up at the heartfelt welcome his friends were once again extending to him. He cleared his throat, then said with a husky voice, "I'm going to go check on the generator and the weather conditions. The ice was supposed to stop sometime late this morning." He stood and walked briskly out of the room and toward the back door.

Guilt is a heavy burden to carry, Sylvia thought, and there is a man who refuses to put it down.

Chapter Thirty

"HOW DARE HE?" Cassandra Weaver fumed as she paced around her suite, eyes not even seeing the homey decor or the warmth the furnishings brought to the space. At the moment, none of that mattered. All that mattered was that her privacy was on the verge of being encroached upon.

The *nerve* of that sheriff even suggesting that he be allowed to search her room was absolutely appalling. How could he think she would just misplace something as valuable as that diamond chain? And what business was it of his whether she brought it on her trip or not? Last time she checked, it was still a free country and people were still allowed to take whatever they wanted with them on vacation.

Even to a place like this.

Staying here had been a mistake. At first staying in an idyllic little town at a bed-and-breakfast in the middle of nowhere sounded appealing. The break from the typical hurried pace of life was just what she needed.

Or so she thought.

That was until she realized last night that she was sharing dinner with a sheriff and his deputy when an ice storm hit, making it impossible for her to get away. Not to mention the Marian Bright woman who owned the place. She was friendly and welcoming, yes, but Cassandra could also tell that not much got past her. She had the intelligent glint in her eyes of someone who's always paying attention to what's going on around her.

How much would she figure out?

Even if she didn't, those intrusive law enforcement guys certainly would if they were able to search her room. She'd hold them off as long as she could, but they'd start to realize she was keeping something from them.

Maybe they already suspected.

Cassandra was a big believer in a person's right to have some secrets. She certainly had her share of them.

The problem was, there were people here who were intent on ferreting them out. What would happen if that sheriff and his deputy had an in with some judge that gave them permission to search her room? What would happen to her once she was found out?

Maybe she should pack up and sneak away like that other couple did. No matter what, she wasn't about to let them find out what she was hiding.

Her life depended on it.

Chapter Thirty-One

"HEY, WAIT FOR me!" Sylvia called after Vito.

He walked briskly toward the new barn he'd built that housed the generator and his tools, slowing his step only when she got his attention.

His stomach clenched at the sight of her. She was so pretty. Even wearing the same thing she did yesterday. "Need something?" he asked, the words coming out sharper than he'd intended.

A fleeting look of surprise crossed Sylvia's face.

"Sorry," he muttered. "I didn't mean it to come out that way."

"That's okay," she assured him. "I just wanted to see if you needed any help."

Vito smirked. "You're not really dressed for manual labor."

She dropped her gaze to the black velvet pants and the luxury wool-blend coat she wore. "No, I guess I'm not. I'm not good at just sitting around, though. I go a little stir-crazy."

A small smile tugged at the corners of Vito's mouth. "After

the breakfast you helped whip up, I'd hardly say you've just been sitting around. It was delicious, by the way."

"Thanks," Sylvia said with a shrug. "I like to cook, though I never cook like that for myself. And anyway, I'd like to help around here any way I can."

"As long as you don't mind ruining your clothes and shoes—and probably your coat—I guess I could find some things for you to do."

Vito watched as Sylvia scrunched her face in thought. He'd love to spend the extra time alone with her, but it could be dangerous. All he needed was to fall even harder for someone who was way out of his league. He was already a goner, but if he was alone with her, he knew he wouldn't stand a chance.

"Well, if it's okay with you, I could borrow some of your clothes…" she suggested, almost shyly. "I promise I'll wash them so I don't make extra work for you."

Vito felt his eyes widen. Sylvia wanted to wear his clothes? A woman hadn't worn anything of his since before Shannon took off with that lawyer. To see Sylvia sporting his flannel would be a step in a direction he was sure would lead them to a dead end. He could picture her with a shirt that was too big for her, the bottom hanging down to her mid-thigh with the sleeves rolled up so she could use her hands. Wearing his clothes was certainly not something a casual acquaintance would do. No, that kind of thing was reserved for a significant other. Or a wife.

Still, he couldn't help himself.

"Sure, I guess that would be fine." Vito's cheeks heated despite the cold air. "We can go to my place to get it real quick before we get to work. You can pick what you want."

Sylvia nodded then fell into step beside him, their feet crunching in unison. "I really appreciate this."

"You know, my stuff isn't nearly as fashionable as yours," he said.

Shrugging, Sylvia stated in a matter-of-fact voice, "Eh, fashion is overrated."

Vito's eyebrows shot toward the edge of his knit cap, and when he looked at her, he saw that she was just as surprised by her remark as he was.

Chapter Thirty-Two

L OUISE HUBLEY STOOD at the window of the suite she shared with her husband and looked out over the dormant garden. "I bet this place is really beautiful in the spring when everything is in bloom."

Grant sat in a deep armchair, the ankle of one leg resting on his other. He held a pipe to his lips and looked every ounce the retired college professor. "I'm sure it is, dear. You seem to like it here."

Turning from the window, Louise crossed her arms loosely over her chest and took a deep breath. "I really do. Other than the robbery, of course. It's just so peaceful out here. It makes me think of how I'd like us to spend our future. Let's get away from the grind, from the commitments and find a quiet place to live. We could grow flowers and vegetables. Maybe even have a dog or two," she said wistfully.

A deep chuckle vibrated Grant's chest. "Who do we look like, Louise? Ma and Pa Ingalls? We've never grown anything in our lives. You've never even been able to keep a houseplant alive. What makes you think we could have a garden? I think the fresh air is going to your head." He took a puff on his pipe and eyed his wife curiously.

"What fresh air?" Louise retorted. "We haven't been outside since the ice started last night. From the looks of things, we won't be going outside any time today and possibly not even tomorrow."

Grant placed his pipe on the small table next to the chair and walked toward her. As he closed the distance between them, he saw the contentment on her face, something he realized he'd never seen before. "What are you saying, Louise?"

"I'm saying that this is the kind of place I don't mind being snowed—or in this case, iced—in. It feels like we've come home."

"Of all the places we've been, *this* is the kind of place you want to settle?" the professor asked incredulously. He waved his hand around the room decorated with rustic furnishings and typical farmhouse decor. "It's peaceful here, I'll give you that, but it certainly lacks the finer things in life that I thought you cared so much about."

Louise shrugged. "Maybe I don't care as much about those things as I thought I did. All I know is that for the first time in a long time, I feel calm, peaceful."

A wave of tenderness for his bride washing over him, Grant reached for Louise and pulled her close. He rested his chin on the top of her head and whispered, "I didn't know you were so unhappy with the life we've been living. I thought it was as thrilling for you as it was for me."

"I didn't know, either. But coming here makes me realize something has to change in our lives. Now that I know something is lacking, I can't go back." Louise buried her face in her husband's chest.

"I'd do anything for you, you know that, but this is something we'll have to discuss."

Louise nodded in agreement. "I know. But what if you retired, I mean *really* retired? No more obligations to anyone, and we just sort of started over. I want a life I feel comfortable in. I guess I never really felt comfortable before. I thought I was, and I was good at playing my role, but maybe I was always meant for something different."

"Point taken," Grant said, then gave his wife a final squeeze before releasing her. "We said we came here on our quest to look at different ways of living, I just didn't think you'd actually find one you liked. At least, not this fast."

The corner of Louise's mouth tugged into a faint smile. "I guess life has a way of surprising us."

"I guess so. So far this trip has been one surprise after another," Grant noted. "It's important to remember that not all surprises are pleasant ones, though, dear."

As Louise turned back toward the window to observe the dormant garden, she could have sworn Grant had just mumbled, "This one sure wasn't."

Chapter Thirty-Three

"WHAT DID THE judge say?" Nadine asked as Joe pushed open the door of Marian's office, Eli on his heels. She was bent over the counter with Ivy, talking quietly about the day's events.

"He wasn't in the cheeriest mood I've ever seen him in. Apparently his power has gone out and his cell phone is dying, so he couldn't spare more than a minute. Despite that, he agreed that we need to get to the bottom of this. He's going to email a makeshift search warrant to me complete with his signature. Now Ms. Weaver will have to cooperate," Joe replied.

"I still don't see her making it easy on us," Eli contradicted. "She'll probably start screaming about police brutality and the rights of private citizens," he concluded, rolling his eyes.

Joe shrugged. "Well, she can take it up with the judge."

"I'm sure she will," the deputy said wryly.

Nadine raised her head from the task she was working on. "Eli, I've never known you to be so cynical."

Eli frowned and pointed in the direction of the guest

rooms. "And I've never known a person to be as uncooperative as that woman. We're trying to solve a crime here, one that she claims to be the victim of, and she won't so much as let us cross the threshold of her suite. What does that say to you?"

Nadine chewed her bottom lip. "Maybe she's had problems with the police in the past. Or maybe she's afraid of men. There could be a lot of reasons." She shrugged for emphasis. Nadine had always been able to see a situation from everyone's point of view. Sometimes it drove Joe nuts. This was one of those times.

"Whatever they are, they don't excuse obstruction of justice," Joe said in his typical matter-of-fact sheriff voice.

"Well, good luck," Nadine said, then gently scolded, "We need you guys to clear out of here so we can get some work done."

"Yes, ma'am," Eli said, slightly tipping his head forward. "We need to have another go of it with Ms. Weaver anyway."

The two men ducked out of the kitchen, letting the door swing behind them as they exited.

"Think a warrant signed by the judge will help?" Eli asked as the two men walked through the sitting room.

"If she doesn't want to be arrested for obstructing justice and tampering with evidence, it will."

Eli stopped mid-stride. The pop and crackle of the fireplace filled the silence. "And what if she still doesn't cooperate? Are you planning to arrest her? Where would you even put her? We're still iced in."

Joe's face scrunched in thought. "Good question. I guess we'd just have to take turns sitting outside her room to make sure she doesn't try to make a run for it."

"And listen to her hurl insults at us through the door? Sounds like a blast," Eli replied dryly.

"Let's just hope she chooses to cooperate so that won't be necessary," Joe said, then turned back in the direction they'd been heading. "Come on. I need you to back me up."

As the two men walked past the front foyer, a thumping sound on the porch stopped them in their tracks. They exchanged looks, then moved in the direction of the noise. Just when they'd reached the front door, it swung inward, two ice-covered figures stepped in from the cold. Ice clung to their coats, eyelashes, and the man's beard. Wind howled behind them.

Joe and Eli blinked to make sure they were seeing correctly. Despite their appearance, the sheriff and his deputy recognized the couple.

It was the Turners.

<h1 style="text-align:center">Chapter Thirty-Four</h1>

"YOU'VE GOT TO be kidding me," Joe snorted as he stared at the two frostbitten figures.

Wes Turner stomped his feet on the doormat, then shucked his jacket and gloves. He bent forward and untied his boots, along with his wife's.

"Do you have any idea the mess you've caused?" Eli scolded, sounding like a frustrated parent. "What were you doing running off in weather like this? You could have frozen to death."

Wes glared at the deputy but remained silent. Eli matched him.

"Wes didn't want to get stuck here with all the ice, so we decided to try to beat the storm," Chrissy said, rubbing her gloved hands together. "We were barely out to the road when it hit. The roads got bad really fast, and we couldn't make it." The young woman shot a glare toward her husband. "He insisted we keep trying, but we slid into a ditch."

"Where did you stay last night?" Joe asked.

Wes gazed at the sheriff with smoldering eyes but didn't answer.

"We bundled up in the car. It was cold, but at least it was shelter. Once it got light, we decided to try getting out of the car and walking back here. Getting the car door open took some doing since ice had frozen over the whole car, but we finally managed." The woman's eyes still watered and her face was red from the cold.

"Take your boots and jackets off, then come sit by the fire. I'll see if I can find any coffee," Eli said, then guided them to the sitting room where they huddled in front of the fireplace. "While I'm doing that, Joe has a few questions to ask you."

Despite being red from the cold, Chrissy blanched. "Questions? For us? What about?"

"We don't have to answer anything," Wes said, speaking for the first time since coming back to the bed-and-breakfast.

"Maybe not," Joe said as his deputy retreated to the kitchen, "but I assure you it would be in your best interest to tell me what I want to know."

"Guess who's here and in need of something hot to drink?" Eli asked when he went back to the kitchen.

Ivy furrowed her eyebrows in confusion. "Who?"

"The Turners," Eli replied, then walked to the coffee pot. "They're both just about frozen stiff and could use some coffee."

Nadine's eyes widened. "They're *back*? Where did they go?" she asked as she retrieved two mugs from the cabinet next to the refrigerator, then handed them to Eli.

The deputy shrugged as he accepted the mugs Nadine held out for him. "Not far, considering the road conditions. According to them, they didn't want to get stuck here and tried to beat the storm. Instead, the storm hit them anyway and they slid into a ditch. They spent the night in their car, then walked back here."

"Did they take Mrs. Hubley's jewelry?" Ivy asked in a conspiratorial tone.

"Joe's questioning them now. I won't know more until I get back in there." He poured coffee into the mugs until the pot was empty. "Would either of you mind making more?" he asked, holding up the now-empty container.

"Sure thing. I'll bring it in when it's ready," Nadine offered, taking the pot from Eli.

Eli cocked an eyebrow at her but said nothing. It wasn't unusual for civilians to become interested in criminal cases. He guessed even Nadine wasn't immune, then shook the thought away. Always hospitable, Nadine was probably just being a good hostess, not a busybody. She'd never given him a reason to think otherwise.

"Okay, whenever it's ready, that would be great," he finally said, then went back to the sitting room where his partner was questioning the suspects in the theft of Louise Hubley's jewelry.

"What exactly are you accusing us of, Sheriff?" Wes Turner asked, his jaw clenching in anger.

"Let's get one thing straight, Mr. Turner. I'm not accusing you of anything. There was a theft last night, right after which you and your wife just happened to disappear. All I want to know is, did you see or hear anything suspicious before you took off last night?" Joe asked, managing to keep his tone civilized.

"Listen here—" Wes began but went silent when his wife placed a hand on his arm.

"We didn't see or hear anything, Sheriff," Chrissy volunteered, "other than the weather report. Wes doesn't like to be stuck one place too long, so we left while we could."

"Thank you for telling us that, Mrs. Turner. So you were already gone when Mrs. Hubley came out of her suite, hysterical that some of her jewelry had gone missing?"

Eli smiled to himself. Joe had gotten so much more civilized during the last two years as sheriff. The approach to witnesses and suspects that was more sledgehammer than kid gloves had softened enough that people were more likely to open up to him.

"She already told you we didn't hear anything," Wes snapped.

Eli stiffened. "Sir, you have to understand that it's the job of law enforcement to ask the same questions in a bunch of different ways to make sure we have all the facts straight. Now, with all due respect, Mr. Turner, you're not being very cooperative. Perhaps if you would try to answer the questions instead of getting defensive, we could get somewhere with this and you could go back to your room to take a hot shower. The longer you take to tell us what we need to know, though, the longer it will be before you're rid of us." The deputy flashed a quick glance at his boss. "And the more likely we are to think you had something to do with the theft."

"I know how it works, Deputy. No, we didn't see or hear anything. We were already gone by the time that Hubley woman started screaming about her jewelry being gone," Wes answered in a more civil tone. "Now, can we please go to our room?"

Joe and Eli exchanged glances, then Joe agreed. "Just make sure you stay put and don't try running off again. We've had two thefts now, and we don't need anybody going missing."

Wes muttered something indistinguishable under his breath, then stood and stalked back to the suite he'd once again be sharing with his wife.

"I'm sorry about my husband," Chrissy Turner whispered. "He's been on the wrong side of the law before, and the things he said were twisted around to make it sound like he did something worse than he really did. He spent a few years in jail because of it. That's why he doesn't like to get stuck in one place for very long."

Joe nodded in understanding. "Makes sense. Thanks for telling us."

Chrissy turned to follow the path her husband had taken, but before she made it more than a few steps away, Eli asked, "Why was he sent to jail?"

The young woman cast her eyes toward the floor. "Theft," she said simply, then turned and walked away.

Chapter Thirty-Five

"CAN WE TALK?" Sylvia asked Nadine in a hushed tone as the two prepared the dough for the sugar cookies the guests would be decorating later. Whispers had been flying around the bed-and-breakfast since the Turners came back, and she didn't want to risk anyone overhearing what she had to say.

"Sure," Nadine replied. "You can talk while we roll out the dough. We're supposed to have the cookie-decorating class in an hour, and I'm running behind."

Sylvia studied her friend. Even with flour on the tip of her nose, she was radiant. It was more than just being pretty, which of course she was. No, Nadine didn't just have a pretty face. She looked…*happy*. She glowed from the inside out.

For the past couple of years Sylvia didn't understand how she and Joe made things work. She was sweet and soft-spoken, always seeing the good in life, and Joe had a grumpy streak that sometimes hung over him like a dark cloud. But somehow the two of them put their differences aside and loved each other in spite of, and maybe because of, those differences.

Rolling pin in hand, Nadine looked up from the lump of cookie dough and, for the first time since Sylvia came into the kitchen, really looked at her friend. "What are you wearing?"

Sylvia dropped her eyes to the baggy flannel shirt and pants that were cinched in at the waist and rolled up above heavy wool socks. "Oh, uh, Vito let me borrow some clothes so I could help him outside. I didn't exactly pack an overnight bag for dinner last night."

Nadine's eyes twinkled. "Vito, huh?"

Heat crept up Sylvia's cheeks. "Yes. Vito."

After watching her friend for a minute, Nadine resumed her task with a vengeance. With nothing else to do while they were all stuck at the Farmhouse Inn, the guests would go stir-crazy and need something to do.

"What did you need to talk to me about?" Nadine asked, never taking her eyes from her work.

Sylvia sorted the cookie cutters next to her friend and hesitated a moment before speaking. "I told him something today that I didn't plan to say. It just sort of slipped out. I have no idea why I'd say something like that."

Nadine stayed focused on her task while asking, "What did you say?"

"I told him that fashion is overrated," Sylvia confessed.

Nadine's hands stilled and she looked at Sylvia, noting the distress on her friend's face. "Overrated? That's your whole career. What did he say?"

Rolling her eyes toward the ceiling, Sylvia blew a stray strand of hair off her forehead. "Nothing. He just looked surprised."

"What were you and Vito doing talking about fashion? He hardly seems the type." Nadine's hands went back to work, then she set the rolling pin aside and straightened the edge of the dough with her hands.

"We weren't exactly talking about fashion. He offered to let me borrow some of his clothes, and said his clothes weren't as fashionable as what I'm used to. That's when I told him fashion is overrated." Sylvia's face oozed misery.

"Interesting," was Nadine's only comment as she reached for a cookie cutter in the shape of a Christmas tree.

Sylvia straightened. "It's not 'interesting.' It's horrible! How could I say such a thing? What would I do with my life if I didn't design clothes?"

Nadine selected a snowman-shaped cookie cutter and looked at Sylvia. She shrugged. "Maybe you're growing up," she suggested.

"I'm in my forties," Sylvia snorted. "How much more growing up can I do?"

Placing the cookie cutter on the counter, Nadine grasped Sylvia's upper arms. "What I mean is, maybe you're beginning to realize that your career isn't everything. I know you've mentioned before that there are areas of your life you feel are lacking. It's possible that those areas are the ones demanding to be satisfied now. You've had an outstanding career and made lots of money, but I get the feeling you're lonely. You even alluded to that last night."

Sylvia nodded in agreement. "Ever since I came to Saddle Hill for the first time two Christmases ago, I've felt at home here. I envied the slower pace you were able to move at. I started to wonder what it would be like to be one of you. I'd hoped that buying a place here would fulfill that need, and while it has provided me a much-needed respite, it's gotten to the point where it doesn't seem like enough. The truth is, I want to live here. Full-time. I don't want to go back to the crush of the crowds in New York. I think I'm ready to live a quiet life."

"Have you talked to your family about this? Your friends in New York?" Nadine asked, releasing Sylvia's arms and picking up the cookie cutter, poising it on the dough before pushing it through.

Sylvia made an exasperated exhale. "I've mentioned it to my mom. She just told me I'm having a midlife crisis."

A giggle escaped Nadine's throat. "This doesn't seem like a midlife crisis to me. It seems to me that you might be ready to make a real change in your life."

"How do I do that?"

"I'd start by thinking about how you want your life to look, and what you'd have to do to get there," Nadine suggested.

"In your opinion, what should I do?" Sylvia pleaded.

A mischievous smile spread across Nadine's face. "My opinion? I think you should grab a cookie cutter and start helping me. We only have half an hour to get these baked and cooled before we invite the guests to come decorate them."

Sylvia smiled in return. "I can do that."

The two friends worked side by side, cutting the cookies and sliding them onto cookie sheets. As the smell of baking cookies soon filled the kitchen, Sylvia knew Nadine was right. This is what she wanted. A slow life, being with her friends in Saddle Hill, and maybe even finding somebody she could share her life with.

Chapter Thirty-Six

"WHY DO YOU always have to be so rude to people?" Chrissy Turner asked her husband.

Wes turned a scowl in her direction. "I'm not rude," he snapped. "You can't trust these people."

Chrissy sighed and lowered herself into one of the over-stuffed chairs in their suite. After spending three years in jail for robbery, Wes was now claustrophobic and trusted no one except her. This was why they'd booked the largest suite at the inn. Could they afford it? No. As the sole income earner and the one who paid the bills, Chrissy was keenly aware of that fact. When Wes felt like the walls were closing in on him, though, he became unbearable. That made the hefty price tag on this trip worth it.

"What's that?" he demanded, pointing toward the paper Chrissy was holding.

"It was under our door when we came back from talking to the sheriff."

Snatching it from her hand, Wes studied it. "They're having

Christmas activities today. Looks like there will be a cookie-decorating class."

Extending her hand, Chrissy asked, "May I please see that?" She was barely able to keep the frustration out of her voice but knew that matching Wes's attitude with one of her own would only escalate his anger further.

She'd already learned that lesson, and it had come with bruises and a busted lip. Unfortunately, she was no stranger to Wes's quick temper.

He thrust the paper in her direction and turned swiftly on his heel and stalked to the bathroom. "I'm going to get a shower," he muttered. The door slammed behind him, the sound of running water following soon after.

Chrissy read over the list of activities being offered today. There was a cookie-decorating class in fifteen minutes.

"I'm going to go to that," she said to no one.

Since Wes got out of jail, her life had been lacking the fun and carefree quality she'd had before. He tried, though. Occasionally he crossed the lines of his comfort zone and did things just to make her happy. This trip was his attempt at trying to do something fun, something she would enjoy.

Decision made, Chrissy stood from the chair and walked toward the bathroom, passing a lovingly decorated Christmas tree on the way. The whole room had been decorated for Christmas. The twinkling lights and the fresh scent of pine gave the place a cozy feeling. It had been a lot of years since she'd felt so welcome in a place. This room and the entire farmhouse felt like a warm hug. The people she'd met here were so friendly, she felt as though she'd known them for a long time.

Too bad Wes insisted that she kept a safe distance from them.

Chrissy knocked on the bathroom door and opened the door slightly. "Wes? I'm going to go to this cookie-decorating class."

"You're what?" he thundered from behind the shower curtain.

"I'm going to the cookie-decorating class," she repeated. "I think it would be fun."

He pulled the shower curtain back slightly and stuck his head out, his beard thick with lather. "I told you to keep your distance from these people. They're already blaming us for stealing that Hubley woman's jewelry."

"They didn't accuse us, Wes," Chrissy contradicted. "They asked us questions, which I'm sure they did to everyone here." She waited a few moments, then added, "I should be allowed to do this since you dragged me out of here during an ice storm and I had to spend the night in a freezing car."

The corners of Wes's mouth drooped. "Fine," he said finally. "But don't expect me to go. And don't say too much." He pulled the shower curtain completely closed again.

She smiled to herself. Maybe things were starting to look up.

Chapter Thirty-Seven

MARIAN BUSTLED AROUND the dining room, setting bowls of the frosting she'd helped Nadine and Sylvia make on the dining room table. Holiday-colored confections had replaced the greenery and candles that decorated the table the night before and at breakfast this morning. Instead of the poinsettias, the red now came from the food coloring in the frosting.

She placed her hands on her hips and took a step back to survey the table. It looked festive with a red-, green-, and white-striped plastic tablecloth. The bowls of candy she'd set out both for snacking and decorating added a fun twist. The buffet table along the wall was set up with carafes of hot chocolate, coffee, and tea. Holiday mugs and bowls of crushed candy canes, marshmallows, and Christmas colored sprinkles completed the preparations.

"Perfect," she said aloud.

Marian smiled. This would be fun.

Taking an otherwise bad situation and turning it into

something good was Marian's specialty. She'd done it last year when she was kidnapped and held hostage in this house, and the year before when she helped clear Kris Jingle's name when he'd been framed for theft.

She looked down at her Christmas sweater. She held to the tradition of wearing a different Christmas sweater for every day of the Christmas season. The one she wore today boasted holly leaves trimming the words *Have Yourself a Merry Little Christmas*.

Despite the cheer it brought her, Marian decided what she wore needed to be even more festive. There were a lot of gloomy folks stuck there and she'd do whatever she could to bring them a little more joy.

Her smile widened. She had just the thing to bring Christmas cheer to everyone there, no matter how grumpy they insisted on being.

Glancing at her watch, she realized she only had a few minutes before the cookie-decorating class began. Though she wasn't a professional pastry chef like Nadine was, she knew her way around a bowl of frosting well enough to help. If she hustled, she'd be back in time to bring a smile to her stranded guests.

Dashing through the kitchen without stopping to talk to Sylvia and Nadine, who were busily sliding the cookies from the cooling rack onto decorative platters, Marian grabbed her coat off the hook beside the door and hurried across the icy ground to her house.

"She was in a hurry," Sylvia observed as Marian sped through the kitchen and out the back door.

Nadine nodded in agreement. "She must have forgotten something at home and needs to get it before the class starts."

Looking at the sugar cookies, baked to a perfect golden brown, Sylvia inhaled the scent. "Those look and smell wonderful!" she said enthusiastically. "How you can bake like this and not weigh three hundred pounds is a miracle."

Smiling, Nadine replied, "I don't bake for me. It's a way to show others that I care."

"Still, I couldn't be around these for long and not eat them by the dozen."

Nadine laughed as she picked up a white platter with Christmas trees around the edge. "Then I guess it's a good thing I've developed some self-control over the years that I've been doing this. It was hard enough to get my body back to normal after Josephine was born. I can't imagine how impossible it would have been if I'd scarfed down cookies and cake."

"Speaking of Josephine," Sylvia said, "once we have everything settled, I should probably give Holly a break. It was so kind of her to take the first shift of babysitting, but I guess I'm up next. Once everything here is settled and everyone is here, I'll take over for her."

Her face drooping into a frown, Nadine said, "I wish I was up next. As soon as this decorating class is over, I'm taking over and spending some time with my girl."

"I'm sure Joe misses her, too," Sylvia said. "Where is he, by the way?"

Nadine shrugged as she walked toward the swinging door that led from the kitchen to the dining room. "I haven't seen him since he and Eli were on their way to question Cassandra

Weaver. I know they got waylaid by the Turners coming back, but I've been so busy I haven't seen him."

Sylvia picked up the other platter of cookies, this one with snowflakes around the edge, and carried them, alongside Nadine, into the dining room. They only had a few minutes until the class started, and thankfully, no one had shown up early. There were a few finishing touches to be made, then they'd be ready.

They placed the trays of cookies on the table, then Nadine snipped a few sprigs from the evergreen wreath that hung on the door to the kitchen and placed them at the corners of each of the platters.

"I hope you didn't leave a bare spot in my wreath," Marian's voice said behind the two women.

When they turned to face her, Sylvia and Nadine burst into laughter. "You're really going all out to make this a festive occasion, aren't you?"

Marian spun in a circle, showing off every angle of the elf costume she'd worn as a mall elf the previous seventeen years. The bells along the hem and on the curved toes of her shoes jingled as she twirled.

"I love it!" Sylvia exclaimed, then wrapped her arms around the older woman.

"How did you sneak up on us with those bells all over you?" Nadine asked.

"Very carefully," Marian replied, her eyes dancing with merriment. "I'm glad I'll still have a use for this costume. To tell the truth, it feels weird not putting it on every day. Wearing it now reminds me of all the joy I brought to the children of Saddle Hill."

"You bring joy to everyone," Sylvia reminded her. "The guests are going to love it."

"I hope so. They're due in here any minute. Let's make this the merriest event ever."

Chapter Thirty-Eight

HOLLY BOUNCED JOSEPHINE up and down on her knee as the baby cooed and giggled. Holly made a funny face, causing the baby to erupt with another round of laughter. Joining the baby's glee, Holly chuckled, too.

She'd never really thought about wanting a baby of her own before, but ever since Josephine was born the idea popped into her head more often than she'd admit. Now that she and Eli were married, they'd been enjoying it being just the two of them. They hadn't even discussed starting a family.

The truth was, Holly didn't even know what she wanted to do. Not really, anyway. Sure, she could watch Josephine and play with her from time to time, but that wasn't the same as having a child that she'd be responsible for all the time. It's not like her mother was some nurturing caregiver that she could emulate. Half the time her mother seemed annoyed that Holly had ever been born.

That's not the kind of thing she'd want to pass on to her own children.

"You look like you're having a good time," Sylvia said from the doorway of the small spare room that had become Josephine's.

Holly smiled. "I am. Josephine is one cool chick. And beautiful, too."

"Of course she is," Sylvia replied. "Look who her mom is."

"Her room looks great!" Sylvia said enthusiastically. She walked to the crib and ran her fingers along the antique frame that had been whitewashed. It now boasted a rustic look that fit perfectly the decor of a farmhouse.

Nodding, Holly agreed. "Vito did a great job in here. From what Marian told me, he did custom molding and woodwork for this room. Said he wanted it to be perfect for Josephine."

Warmth washed up Sylvia's chest. "That was very sweet of him to do for her." It was so rare that someone would put that much effort into a room for a baby. Especially a baby that wasn't his. That spoke volumes to Sylvia about the kind of man he was.

Holly cradled the girl in her arms and walked over to Sylvia. "Look who's here to see us," Holly crooned. "Does Auntie Sylvie want some snuggles?"

The baby extended her arms toward Sylvia before she propelled herself in Sylvia's direction. Sylvia caught her, then gently scolded, "You've got to wait till I'm ready. I don't want to drop you." She turned her attention to Holly. "I'm here to take over. You can go have some adult conversation. You can even go decorate cookies if you want. I'm pretty sure we made plenty."

Holly yawned. "Thanks. She's cute, but she's exhausting. I don't see how Nadine and Joe do it. Both have jobs and also take care of this little bundle of energy. Once she starts walking, they'll be run ragged."

"They certainly will," Sylvia agreed as she nuzzled Josephine's neck. "It probably helps that they are completely in love with this little thing."

Holly scowled. "I love her, too, but she wears me out."

Sylvia bounced the baby on her hip. "I know, but I'm sure it's different when it's your own child. You'll see one day when you and Eli start having kids."

Nodding slowly, Holly muttered, "Yeah, whenever that is. I hope we can handle it."

"Don't be silly. I've seen you with Josephine. You're a great aunt, and you'll be a great mom."

"I hope so," Holly said, but doubted that Sylvia's words were true. She stretched her back then added, "I think I will go decorate some cookies. I could use some sugar."

"Put one aside for me," Sylvia called at her friend's back as she left the room. Despite the demands of her career to look good and stay trim, all she wanted right now was to eat a half dozen of Nadine's marvelous cookies.

For the second time that day, the thought that fashion is overrated crept into her mind.

What is going on with me? Sylvia wondered, still troubled by what she'd said to Vito and the thought that had now lodged itself in her brain.

If this was some sort of midlife crisis, she needed to get over it, pronto.

But if it wasn't, it might be time to consider some major life changes.

Chapter Thirty-Nine

HAPPY CHATTER FILLED the dining room as the guests of the Farmhouse Inn Bed & Breakfast were seated around the table, each with small bowls of various colors of frosting and several cookies in front of them. Courtesy of Ivy, mugs of hot chocolate, coffee, and tea stayed full and sat next to each person.

"This is more fun than I thought it would be," Kris Jingle declared as he plucked a cookie in the shape of a Santa hat off one of the platters.

"I guess you're not the Christmas grump your father and brother always thought you were," his mother quipped, spreading green frosting on her own cookie in the shape of a Christmas tree. "And look at what you're decorating. Here we all thought you hated being Santa."

Kris cast a quick glance at Ivy before frowning at his mother. "No, I'm not a Christmas grump. And I didn't hate being Santa at the mall. It was the excess materialism I had a problem with. Those kids' lists just kept getting longer and longer. It's like they were never satisfied." The familiar shade of red that crept toward his receding hairline betrayed his embarrassment.

James Jingle studied his wife's Christmas tree cookie. "Patty, that doesn't look like the cookies you used to make."

Patricia stole a quick glance at Nadine, who was chewing her lip. A brief look at her amused son communicated to her that her secret was moments from being brought out into the open.

The truth was, Patricia hadn't made Christmas cookies in over a decade. She'd struck a deal with Nadine years ago, paying her under the table to keep her husband's Christmas cookie habit satisfied. For years, it had been a secret only between Patricia and Nadine. A couple Christmases ago, though, Patricia had let her son in on the charade.

Now she was left to wonder if Kris would choose this moment to get back at his mom for embarrassing him in front of everyone else.

Kris cleared his throat. "Well, you know, Dad," he began while his mom shot him a pleading look. "She's probably out of practice. Since you stopped celebrating Christmas year-round, I'm sure she hasn't been baking nearly as many of them."

The elder Jingle thought quietly for a moment. "That's probably true," he agreed. "My waistband says that I haven't eaten nearly as many as I used to. My doctor is pretty happy about it, too."

Mouthing a silent "thank you" to her son, Patricia carried on with her decorating.

Nadine walked around the table, offering praise and advice to the guests. "Carla, you want to outline that gingerbread man with a thinner strip of icing. If it's too thick, it just looks gloppy."

Carla Stockton looked up from her task into the caring eyes of their resident baking expert. "What can I say? I like frosting." She patted her pudgy midsection and asked, "Can't you tell?"

Nadine laughed and moved on to Ralph. "That looks good enough to eat, Ralph. You're doing a wonderful job."

"This is nothing compared to the steady hand it requires to set diamonds," he declared, never taking his eyes from the snowman he was decorating.

"Mrs. Turner, I hope you're having fun," Nadine said carefully. "It's too bad your husband couldn't join us."

"Oh, I'm having a blast. Trust me, it's a lot more fun without him. He's not exactly the jolly sort, and learning how to decorate cookies isn't really his thing." Chrissy turned her snowflake cookie around for Nadine to see. "How'd I do?"

"That looks great!" Nadine enthused. "Keep it up, and you'll give me a run for my money."

Chuckling, Chrissy objected. "Somehow I doubt that. But it is a lot of fun."

Nadine continued making her rounds, stopping at Grant Hubley. "Professor Hubley, that looks really good. Maybe you found your next career. I'm just sorry your wife couldn't make it. I think she would have enjoyed it."

"Yes, Louise would have liked this. I'm afraid she seems to be having some kind of personal crisis, though, and doesn't feel much like being around people at the moment. She has a lot on her mind."

"I understand," Nadine said, tightening her lips and nodding. "I'm sure she's having a tough time after the theft."

There were several moments of awkward silence that threatened to dampen the festive atmosphere.

"I'm afraid I'm not much for the cookie decorating," Holly confessed, breaking the tension. "But I can bake them and eat them."

A chorus of, "I'm good at eating them," and "Can't you tell I'd rather eat them than decorate them?" sounded around the table.

The occasion turned out to be as festive and cheerful as Marian had hoped, and the jingle bells on her elf costume only brightened the mood even more.

When the hour-long lesson was up, crumbs and small mounds of frosting littered the table and floor.

"Remember to come back in two hours for our next holiday lesson. We'll be teaching you how to make Christmas cards," Marian announced as the guests stood from their chairs and collected the cookies they'd decorated. "Feel free to take your mugs back to your room with you, but please make sure you bring them back to the kitchen. We'll leave the drinks out in case you want a refill."

After many murmured *thank yous*, the crowd dispersed, guests returning to their rooms and the residents that had gotten stuck there adjourning to the sitting room. It had been a fun time together and getting to know a couple of the guests. The unspoken hope that nothing else would go wrong glowed on everyone's faces.

Despite, or possibly because of, the ice storm, it would be a Christmas everyone would remember for a long time.

Chapter Forty

JOE AND ELI sat across from a stone-faced Cassandra Weaver in her suite while they attempted to question her about the theft of her jewelry. The small Christmas tree twinkling on the top of the dresser did nothing to thaw her frosty mood. Sitting with her lips drawn tight and her arms folded across her chest, the disapproval radiating from her was palpable.

"I just want to make it known that I'm cooperating against my will," Cassandra ground out.

"Noted," Joe replied shortly. "You have made that perfectly clear."

"The fact that you went behind my back and got a warrant from a judge when you were fully aware that I didn't wish for this to go any further speaks volumes about the kind of men you are. I will make it known that the law enforcement in this town cannot be trusted," she huffed.

"Ma'am, I don't think we need to remind you that you were allegedly a victim of theft. The fact that you are not cooperating with us makes us question whether or not a theft actually occurred. Surely you understand our dilemma," Eli said in a tone that invited cooperation.

Still Ms. Weaver stood firm. "I assure you that a theft happened, but shouldn't it be my right whether or not I let you snoop around my room?" she asked indignantly.

"Ma'am, I assure you we aren't snooping," Joe said through clenched teeth. "We have an obligation to uphold the law and see that justice is done. If a crime has been committed, it's our responsibility to find out what happened and who committed it. That's what we're trying to do. Please believe us when we say we have no interest in looking through your stuff for any other reason."

Standing from her chair, Cassandra said, "I'll have to think about it. If you would be so kind as to give me time to do that in private, I would appreciate it. In the meantime, you might want to consider searching everyone else on the premises. I assure you that you'll find my diamond chain, and quite possibly whatever was stolen from that professor's wife." She walked to the door of her suite and opened it. "Now, if you'll excuse me."

Joe and Eli exchanged annoyed glances then stood and walked to the door. Before turning to leave, Eli said, "We have a warrant, Ms. Weaver, and we're giving you this time as a courtesy. By law, we have the right to conduct this search right now. Think that over while you're accusing us of, quote, snooping."

After the door clicked shut behind them, Joe shook his head and Eli blew out a heavy exhale.

"Is it just me," Eli said, "or is that woman hiding something?"

Chapter Forty-One

VITO TAPPED ON the door of Josephine's small room and was pleased when Sylvia greeted him.

"Vito. Hi," Sylvia said in surprise when she opened the door. Josephine was perched on her hip, a clump of her hair clutched in the baby's chubby hand.

"Hello," he responded, a smile wrinkling the skin around his eyes. "Looks like she's fixing your hair for you."

Sylvia chuckled lightly. "She can't make it look much worse than it already does. All my stuff to fix it is at home."

Shrugging, Vito said playfully, "Fashion is overrated anyway, right?"

She pinched her lips together. "Apparently." Sylvia glanced around the room. "You did a really nice job with this room. Nadine told me it used to be a storage room, and Holly told me about the extra work you put into this room to make it nice for Josephine."

Nodding in agreement, Vito replied, "It did." He motioned toward the window above the crib. "There wasn't originally a window there, but I thought this little lady could use the sun-shine. She also needed something more interesting than just plain walls, so I added some trim and woodwork. Things that are visually interesting are good for a baby's brain development." He extended his hand toward the baby, and she grabbed hold of his index finger, then tried to put it in her mouth.

"You're good with her," Sylvia observed.

He shrugged. "I like kids, and for whatever reason, they seem to like me, too."

"Maybe that's because you take the time to make sure they have amazing bedrooms," she said with a smile. "I don't get much time with kids. Since my clothing line is for adults, that's all I ever see," Sylvia admitted.

"I actually wanted to talk to you about that," he said, a serious look replacing the amusement that had been there moments before.

A frown furrowed Sylvia's forehead. "What about it?" she asked cautiously.

Vito took a step forward and settled into the rocking chair near Josephine's crib. "It just seems like something is bothering you. When I first met you last year, you walked with your chin up and oozed confidence. These days, I don't know, it just seems like something is weighing you down."

The concern in his voice warmed Sylvia, but what would happen if she made him a confidante? She was already keenly aware of her feelings for him, and she suspected he felt the same way. Spilling her guts to him about how torn she felt between her career and her personal life would only complicate things and could very possibly allow him to get closer than she was ready for.

Still, it would be nice to have a man's opinion on the matter. She could always talk to Joe, Eli, or Ralph, she supposed, but she knew them too well. Besides, all of them were already married and would give their opinion based on what it was like to be married. And none of them had to walk away from an incredibly lucrative career to balance their personal and professional lives.

She would, and she couldn't take any more of the "follow-your-heart" comments from Nadine and Holly. Sylvia's heart was no help at all in the matter and pulled her in two different directions. She loved her job but also yearned for something more.

"If you don't want to talk about it, that's okay," Vito finally said after Sylvia had been lost in her ruminations for several minutes. "I just thought it might help to talk about whatever's weighing on you."

"No, it isn't that," Sylvia said hurriedly. "I was just trying to decide how much to share. I mean, we don't know each other that well."

Vito shifted in his chair and made a move to stand up. "I'm sorry if I've crossed a line. That wasn't my intention."

"Oh gosh, no!" She turned toward the crib and lowered Josephine into it, placing the baby's favorite rattle in her pudgy fingers. She turned back to face Vito, and conceded, "It actually would be nice to get some things off my chest."

At that, Sylvia launched into her dilemma about work taking too much of her time and stated that she was now at the age where she just wanted things to slow down.

"What do you think that would look like?" Vito asked when Sylvia paused long enough for him to speak.

Sylvia sighed heavily and sank into the deep, cozy chair that occupied the wall on the opposite side of Josephine's crib. "That's just it. I have no idea. How could I possibly walk away from an entire clothing line that *I* started? But how can I just keep ignoring the other parts of my life that have nothing to do with work?"

Vito leaned forward in his chair and rested his elbows on his knees. "Does it have to be either/or? Can't you have both?"

Her mouth curved into a sad, wry smile. "That's what everybody says. People say we can have it all. The truth is, though, making the choice to do both pretty much guarantees that one or the other will suffer. I've been realizing lately that humans weren't meant to do it all, and that the older—and, hopefully, wiser—we get, the less we *want* to do it all. That seems to be the case with me, anyway. I've been successful in my career, and I kind of want to see what else is out there."

Vito nodded and appeared to be thinking through the things she said.

"I know I was rambling. I'm sorry," Sylvia said, embarrassed that she'd bared so much of her soul to a man she didn't know all that well.

"You weren't rambling," Vito said softly. "Have you talked to Ralph about any of this? He has an interest in whether or not you continue with your career. He's still the jewelry designer for your line, isn't he?"

Sylvia nodded and chewed on her lower lip. How thoughtless of her to not even consider Ralph. On the brink of losing his store just a couple years ago, his partnership with Jersey Belle assured him financial security for as long as their collaboration lasted. If she were ever to step back from Jersey Belle, she'd be putting that security at risk.

"I hadn't even thought about talking to him about it. It's so easy to think of him as a friend more than a business associate. You're right. I shouldn't make any decisions without talking to him." The corners of Sylvia's mouth tilted up slightly. "You're good at this," she told Vito.

He shrugged and stood from the rocking chair. "Just trying to help. Let me know if you need to think through things again." He turned to leave the room, then paused and glanced over his shoulder. "You look good with a baby on your hip," he said with a mischievous smile, then opened the door and left.

When he was gone, Sylvia glanced down at Josephine, who was playing happily with her rattle. A twinge of pain clenched her heart. She did look good with a baby on her hip. She felt good, too.

Now if only there was a way to have her career and a family at the same time.

Chapter Forty-Two

"SHE MIGHT BE hiding something, but she's not wrong," Joe admitted to his deputy. "Now that we've had another robbery, we really should get another warrant to check everyone else's rooms again to see if Ms. Weaver's diamonds turn up. And to search her room to see if there is any actual evidence that a robbery occurred."

"Her jewelry did go missing once the Turners came back. According to her, anyway," Eli observed aloud. "Maybe we should check their room first."

"Might not be a bad idea," Joe agreed. "I'll need to call the judge first and ask him to sign another warrant that will let us do a broader search."

"Good luck," Eli said with a snort.

"Thanks. Judge Becker won't be happy."

Eli shook his head. "It's crazy, isn't it? This is the third Christmas in a row that crime has come to Saddle Hill after—what, a decade of nothing? We just came for dinner, and now we're stuck here because of an ice storm, investigating jewel theft."

"You said it," Joe muttered under his breath. "Two out of the last three Christmases have involved jewel theft. What's happening to our town?"

Shrugging, Eli said, "I'm going to go to the kitchen and see if there are any cookies left over while you call the judge."

As he pulled his phone from his back pocket and headed once again for Marian's office, Joe called, "Save one for me if there are," at Eli's retreating back.

With a thumbs-up over his shoulder, Eli disappeared into the kitchen, the smell of sugar cookies baked to perfection wafting through the swinging door.

"Judge Becker, it's Joe Adler," the sheriff said into the phone when the judge answered.

An exasperated voice on the other end of the call greeted him. "Sheriff, I trust this isn't more business I can't do anything about."

Joe cleared his throat, acutely aware of the judge's reputation for having little patience with people who bothered him.

"Well, Your Honor, we've had another robbery at the Farmhouse Inn, and I need a warrant that has a broader scope. I need to be able to search everyone's rooms and look through their bags and other personal belongings."

"Another robbery? What kind of place is Marian running out there? And what kind of law enforcement officials does this town have that allows not one, but two thefts?" the judge growled.

Joe felt his ears turning red. He had to bite his tongue to keep from telling Judge Becker that none of this was his fault.

"Sir, with all due respect, Marian's bed-and-breakfast is a great place. Unfortunately, she has a guest with sticky fingers. Deputy Nolan and I will work in shifts tonight to make sure nothing else is taken," Joe assured him.

"How about the latest victim?"

"Well, to be honest, she's not the most cooperative one we've ever had. She refuses to let us help her. Keeps complaining about us hassling her—which we absolutely aren't doing. That's part of why we need a broader search warrant. She won't let us have access to the crime scene, and we can't solve this without it."

Joe listened to shuffling on the other side of the call.

"Listen, Sheriff, I've got enough problems without you adding to them. My pipes are busted and my freezer is on the skids. Fortunately, it's cold enough outside that I can put my food out there and it should be fine. With my luck, a bear will come by and eat it all then wreck my house trying to get in," the judge groused. "Granting your request, even once, let alone twice, is highly unusual. Given the circumstances, though, I'll send another warrant, but you better make sure this is the last one you need."

"Yes, Your Honor. I'm sorry about your pipes and freezer. I'll find out who is behind these robberies. You have my word."

The silence stretching between the two men communicated that the judge wasn't so sure Joe would hold up his end of the deal.

I'll just have to prove him wrong, Joe thought, determination fortifying his spirit.

When the judge continued to stay silent, Joe checked the screen of his phone.

Judge Becker had ended the call.

Now all he could do was wait for the warrant to come through, then he'd be able to search Cassandra Weaver's room to see if there was any evidence that she had, in fact, been the victim of a robbery. Unfortunately, his gut told him that any evidence there'd been had been tampered with.

He shook his head. What was that woman up to?

Chapter Forty-Three

"OW'S IT GOING out there?" Holly asked her husband after he planted a kiss on the top of her head.

"Cassandra Weaver isn't cooperating. Joe is calling the judge now for another warrant," Eli replied as he plucked an expertly decorated cookie from the tray on the kitchen island. "Nadine must have decorated this one," he said, taking a large bite, crumbs tumbling down the front of his shirt.

"As a matter of fact, I decorated that one," Holly protested.

"Get out of here," Eli said, looking from Holly to Nadine.

"No, she really did," Nadine affirmed. "The girl has a knack for confections. You better watch out or you'll get that spare tire married men are so famous for."

Eli looked down at his waistline and patted his stomach. "So far, so good," he said, satisfied that his stomach was still as flat as it had been before they were married.

Marian sailed into the kitchen, her elf costume jingling with every step she took. "What's going on in here?" she asked as she went straight for the coffee pot. After pouring a generous mugful, she faced her friends and said, "I don't normally drink this much coffee, but it would seem that these aren't normal circumstances." With that, she took a big gulp of the coffee and joined the group.

"Eli was just telling us that Cassandra Weaver isn't cooperating with their investigation concerning the theft of her jewelry," Nadine said, filling Marian in on what had been going on.

"That's ridiculous," Marian quipped. "Why would a victim not be willing to let the sheriff investigate a crime against her?" She slid her backside onto a stool at the counter and took a cookie shaped and decorated like a Christmas wreath from the platter.

"Joe is calling the judge now to get a warrant that will allow us to search everyone's room and their belongings. Hopefully he'll grant that request and we can move on with it," Eli volunteered as he polished off the last of the cookie. He reached for another but Holly stopped him.

"Remember that spare tire Nadine was talking about? Let's not find out how many cookies it will take to develop one," Holly said, a twinkle in her eye.

"Why is this happening the first Christmas we've been open?" Marian asked, more forlorn than anyone had ever heard her. "Why would somebody go on vacation, then steal someone else's jewelry?" She took another drink of coffee and sighed.

Holly grasped one of Marian's hands and gave it a squeeze. "I don't know why this is happening. Somebody thinks they have a right to someone else's things. A person's reasons for stealing are personal."

Silence fell over the group as each one remembered that

Holly had experience in the matter. Before coming to Saddle Hill, she'd been arrested for shoplifting more than once. Then, once she came to Saddle Hill, her disappearance right after Ralph Stockton's Christmas star had been stolen cast suspicion on her.

She released Marian's hand and shifted uncomfortably on her feet. "I know what you all are thinking. That I'm the only one here who would know anything about why a person would steal. Unfortunately, that's true, but as you all know, I put that behind me a couple years ago. I haven't even been tempted."

Marian rubbed the younger woman's back with her thin hand. "Nobody thinks you have anything to do with the thefts here, dear. Let the past stay in the past."

Nadine and Eli nodded in agreement. "Nobody thinks you had anything to do with it," Nadine assured her while Eli slyly said, "I'll keep a close eye on you, just in case." He winked at his new wife, who rewarded him with a smile.

"I've missed you, too," Holly replied to her husband.

Everyone turned their attention toward the sound of footsteps coming from Marian's office.

"Doesn't look like much Christmas cheer is happening in here," Joe said once he joined the group. He snagged a cookie off the tray and took a bite, relishing his wife's handiwork. "Nobody bakes like you, Nay," he said, a note of admiration in his words.

Nadine raised a shoulder and let it drop. "I don't know. Holly is trying to give me a run for my money."

"It's hard to have Christmas spirit when someone is running around here stealing stuff," Eli said, bemoaning the situation they all found themselves in.

"Well, it could be worse," Joe informed them. "Judge Becker's pipes are busted and his freezer went out. Now he's certain bears are going to be coming to eat the food he's put outside."

"At least our pipes are fine, thanks to the extra insulation Vito had the foresight to install when he was renovating this old place," Marian said, her face glowing with appreciation at their good fortune.

"How did your call go with the judge?" Eli asked, steering them back on topic. "Other than the busted pipes and bum freezer?"

"He'll send me a warrant. I'm just waiting for it. It should include wording that lets us search everyone's room and look through their personal belongings. Fingers crossed that we find something," Joe said, taking another bite of his cookie.

Nadine brought her husband a cup of coffee, and he raised the mug in a mock toast to the season. "May the thief be caught, the ice melt, and the Christmas season continue without anything else going wrong."

"Hear, hear!" Everyone cheered and raised their mugs to meet Joe's, despite the sinking feeling in the pits of their stomachs that things would go the exact opposite of what they'd just toasted.

Chapter Forty-Four

HAVING BEEN RELIEVED of her babysitting duties when Nadine had finished in the kitchen, Sylvia found Ralph and Carla sitting by the fireplace in the sitting room, each with a cup of hot chocolate in their hands.

"It sure looks cozy in here," she observed as she took a seat in a chair across from them. "The two of you sitting here with hot chocolate looks like a scene from a Christmas movie."

Carla laughed. "And with everything that's been going on around here, we could very easily be living the plot of one. Of course, everything would have to work out in the end. The jewelry would be recovered, the thief caught, then seeing the error of his—or her—ways, would end up becoming a pillar of the community. Add, of course, that someone would have to fall in love at the end."

Ralph chuckled. "All these new movies are basically the same, aren't they?"

"They found a formula that works. You can't fault them for using it over and over again," Carla said thoughtfully.

Sylvia saw her opening and cleared her throat. "Speaking of a formula that works, would you be open to talking a little business, Ralph?"

"Sure," he responded, placing his mug on the coffee table in front of him.

Carla hoisted herself off the sofa she'd been sharing with Ralph. "That's my cue. I'll just go into the kitchen and see what the others are up to."

"I thought you were on vacation," Ralph said in a questioning tone.

"I am, but I need to talk to you about work for a couple of minutes."

Ralph studied her for a minute before speaking. Finally, he said, "Something's bothering you."

Sylvia pursed her lips. "Am I that transparent? You're the second person today to say that."

"What's the problem? Has something come up at work?" Concern creased Ralph's face as he spoke.

"No, nothing like that," Sylvia assured him. "It's just…"

The jeweler watched her as she shifted uncomfortably in her seat. "What is it, Sylvia?"

She chewed on her bottom lip as she tried to decide what to say. "How do you know what to do when something that used to be right for you suddenly feels wrong?"

Ralph's eyebrows dipped into a frown. "Are you having some kind of midlife crisis? Because if you are, I'm here to tell you that those can be miserable. I'm convinced that I was having one when I married Brenda. Why else would I have hitched my wagon to someone that didn't share any of my values?"

Sylvia shook her head. "The best thing you've ever done in life was cut ties with her."

Ralph's first wife, Brenda Morris-Stockton, had been a college classmate of Sylvia's. Always trying to make herself look better, she'd teased Sylvia mercilessly about her frizzy hair and the weight she never seemed to be able to lose.

With a visible shudder, Ralph reminisced, "In some ways, I still find it hard to believe that she actually *stole* from me. I mean, what kind of person would steal from her own husband? But she's still sitting in jail while I'm married to the love of my life with a lucrative partnership with one of the most well-known name brands in women's fashion."

Sylvia winced. "That's sort of what I wanted to talk to you about."

Ralph's face paled. "Are you thinking of dissolving our partnership? Are you unhappy with my designs?" he panicked.

"Oh goodness! No! And I don't think I'm having a midlife crisis." Sylvia stood from her chair and crossed over to the sofa, taking the spot Carla had occupied.

Leaning away from her slightly, he said, "You're making me nervous. Will you please just come out with it?"

Inhaling deeply, Sylvia plunged into her dilemma. "My career is great. I'm so thankful for the opportunities it's given me. I love the work of designing and helping people feel great about how they look. The problem is, I feel like I'm missing something. I'm in my forties, and I'm unmarried with no kids. For a long time, I thought that didn't matter and that my career was enough. Now I've realized I was wrong."

"Ah, yes. You've finally reached the level of maturity where you realize money and career isn't everything," Ralph noted, his eyes dancing with amusement. "I remember when that hap-pened to me. Unfortunately, I ran off and married the exact wrong woman."

"So, what should I do?" Sylvia pleaded, hoping Ralph's accumulated wisdom would help her.

"I assume you don't want to hear 'Follow your heart'?"

Rolling her eyes, Sylvia retorted, "That would be all well and good if my heart wasn't pulling me in two opposite directions."

"I figured as much," Ralph said with a knowing smile. "What about your second-in-command at Jersey Belle? Do you trust her?"

The question startled Sylvia. "Of course I do. Otherwise she wouldn't be second-in-command."

Ralph was quiet for several long moments as he thought. "Then why don't you come up with a plan to split more of the responsibilities with her? Give her a pay raise, and of course you'd have to dock your own pay to make up the difference. If you're sharing responsibilities, you should also share the money."

Sylvia watched the flames dancing in the fireplace as she considered what Ralph said. That was one of the things she liked and respected most about him. He wasn't caught up in the glitz of high fashion the way so many in her world were. He had an almost uncanny ability to see all sides of a situation—and, of course, he was right about this, too.

What she really wanted was to spend at least half her time in Saddle Hill, breathing in the fresh, country air and settling into a quieter life—one the city didn't offer. She didn't need as much money as she currently made to live the kind of life she wanted.

"I'd still want creative control of the designs, though," she thought aloud. "It's the day-to-day stuff in the office that I'd like to distance myself from. Do you think I could do the design work remotely?"

Ralph smiled at his beautiful friend. "It's your company. You can do whatever you want." His statement was rewarded with soft laughter.

"Yes, I suppose I can," she agreed, feeling that the weight of her decision had been somewhat lifted.

"Good. Then that's settled. Does this mean that I'm not in danger of being tossed out on my ear?" he said, mostly joking but still looking for some assurance that his partnership with Jersey Belle remained secure.

"You're in no danger," Sylvia promised, then wrapped her arms around Ralph's ample frame. "And thank you for the wise counsel."

Ralph returned the hug. "Anytime."

Sylvia stood and said, "I think I'll go see if there's anything I can help with in the kitchen. From what I gather, Marian has a whole day of Christmas festivities planned."

Ralph heaved himself off the sofa behind her. "I'll help, too. I know you can't tell by looking at me, but I'm not used to sitting around all day."

As the two friends walked toward the kitchen, Sylvia walked a little lighter with the possibility that she might be able to have the life she wanted, after all.

Chapter Forty-Five

"CAN I DO something to help?" Kris asked Ivy as she set up the buffet in the dining room for the next Christmas event.

"If you wouldn't mind carrying that back to the kitchen, I'd appreciate it," Ivy answered as she tucked a strand of her chin-length hair behind her ear. "I need to clean and refill it for the Christmas card-making class."

Kris grasped the stainless-steel drink dispenser by the handles and lifted it off the buffet. "Marian sure is going all out trying to make being iced in festive," he said as he turned toward the door to the kitchen.

"You're telling me. She's going to wear us out with all the merriment," Ivy complained, following him toward the kitchen, balancing bowls of toppings from the hot chocolate bar in her hands. "But I'm sure it's good for business, and leave it to Marian to make the best of a bad situation."

Kris set the drink dispenser on the counter with a clang. "She's good at that. When we worked together, she always reminded me to put on a smile for the kids. It's easy to be happy around her."

Ivy nodded as she placed the bowls near the dispenser. "I wish I was more like that. I try my best to see the good in things, but sometimes it's hard, you know?"

Turning to face her, Kris placed a hand on the counter. "Yeah. I'm a work in progress, too. I spent my whole life being viewed as the Grinch by my whole family. They thought I hated Christmas and never missed an opportunity to poke fun at me."

Ivy shook her head. "I can't even imagine living in a home where you're forced to live like it's Christmas three-hundred-sixty-five days a year. That must have been awful. What did you do in the summer? Weren't the clothes hot?"

An unexpected chuckle escaped Kris's throat. "It sure was. Dad always had sweat stains under his arms, but he refused to wear anything else, even in July."

Working to prepare a fresh batch of hot cocoa, Ivy measured and poured and stirred and whisked until the chocolaty drink was frothy and fragrant while Kris refilled the bowls with crushed candy canes, mini marshmallows, red and green sprinkles, and whipped cream.

"This sure is a lot of stuff to mix into hot chocolate," he said as he replaced the spoons in each bowl. "Even though all this sugar would probably put me into a coma, it does look fun and festive. And delicious, which I guess is what Marian is going for."

After replacing the lid on the drink dispenser, Ivy turned back to Kris. "Would you mind carrying this back into the dining room? It's a little heavy for me, and I can't imagine anything worse than dropping it on the freshly waxed floor in there."

"Sure thing," he agreed as she gathered the refilled bowls.

"You're right about this being a lot of sugar. Some people love it, though. Personally, I prefer a plain cup of tea," she confided.

Kris smiled as they took the things back to the dining room. Ivy was as easy to talk to as she was cute and seemed to have a good head on her shoulders. He felt like he could be himself around her, which is something he'd never experienced.

Maybe when all this nonsense was over and they were allowed to leave the bed-and-breakfast, he'd ask her to have lunch with him.

It was Christmas, after all, and miracles have been known to happen at Christmas.

Chapter Forty-Six

"I BROUGHT THIS FOR you," Chrissy Turner said to her husband as she extended her hand. In it she held a cookie in the shape of a reindeer, which she'd decorated herself at the cookie-decorating class.

"A cookie?" Wes asked sharply.

"Yeah, a cookie. I decorated it at the class." Chrissy's voice sounded wary, as though she was afraid her husband might fly off in a rage.

With a cautious look, he accepted the cookie and took a bite. He nodded in approval. "This is actually pretty good. Better than prison food, I'll tell ya that much."

Chrissy felt as if a weight had been lifted from her shoulders. Since he'd gotten out of jail, Wes had been so surly and hard to please, not to mention hard to live with. Unable to stay in one place for more than a few days for fear of feeling trapped, it had been impossible for her to form any meaningful friendships or put down roots. With Wes being as quiet as he was, she'd be lying if she said she wasn't lonely.

"Wes, why don't you come to the next class with me?" she ventured. "They're teaching us to make Christmas cards from scratch so we don't always have to rely on stores having ones we like."

Wes grunted. "Wouldn't you have to get the supplies at the store, anyway? Seems to me it would be easier to just buy ones that are already made."

Chrissy shrugged. "I guess so, but wouldn't it be fun to get out of this room and do something?" she challenged. "You say you feel caged in when you're stuck in one spot too long, but here you are making yourself stay in one spot. It doesn't make sense."

"It makes perfect sense," he objected. "You know I don't trust these people. Especially that sheriff and his deputy. I know they're going to find a way to pin that woman's missing jewelry on me."

The young woman glanced around their suite. It was the largest one at the Farmhouse Inn and was festively decorated with a Christmas tree, a wreath on the door, poinsettias—there was even a lit garland on the mantle of the fireplace. This was to be a dream getaway, just the two of them, without a care in the world. Instead, her husband had practically dragged her out of there when he found out law enforcement officials would be staying the night. No matter how much she'd tried to talk sense into him, he wouldn't listen.

Now here they were, Chrissy trying to make herself part of the small community, even if it was for only a couple days, and Wes trying to avoid social interaction altogether.

"Please, Wes," she asked. "Can't we do something fun together? Something normal couples would do? Something we would have done together before you went to jail?" In a last-ditch effort to force some fun on her husband, she added, "Don't you think you owe me that much after almost making us freeze to death last night?"

Wes's eyes smoldered. "You know I'd never let anything happen to you. We came back here, didn't we?"

"Only because the only other choice was freezing to death," Chrissy countered. "Otherwise, who knows where we'd be. I need friends, Wes. Even though these people won't be in my life for more than a few days, they can be friends while we're here."

His shoulders sagged as though all the fight had been knocked out of him. "Fine. We'll go learn how to make Christmas cards and get you some of that human interaction you care so much about."

Chrissy squealed and threw her arms around her husband's neck. "Thank you! It will be fun, and you might even surprise yourself by enjoying it. Just make sure you behave yourself," she cautioned playfully.

"Cross my heart," he said while doing the motion across his chest with his hand.

"You're a good man, Wes Turner," she told her husband, still hugging him around the neck.

The moment between husband and wife was interrupted by a pounding on the door.

"Sheriff!" a voice called from the hall. "I have a warrant to search your room. Open up!"

The light moment between Wes and Chrissy tensed as he made a move to open the door. Placing a hand on Wes's forearm, Chrissy stopped him. It was hard to know how Wes would react once he was face-to-face with the sheriff.

Whispering a quick prayer, Chrissy opened the door and invited the sheriff and his deputy inside.

They wouldn't find anything in this room. Would they?

Chapter Forty-Seven

WITH THE SIGNED and emailed search warrant pulled up on the screen of his phone, Joe knocked loudly on the door to Wes and Chrissy Turner's suite. He and Eli looked at each other.

"I can only imagine how Wes Turner is going to react to this," Eli said under his breath.

"I know. I hope your training in hand-to-hand combat is fresh in your mind," Joe replied quietly as the door to the suite swung open.

Standing before them was Chrissy Turner, her face pinched with worry. "Please tread lightly here," she requested. "Wes has a hard time trusting law enforcement."

Joe nodded slightly, then said in a friendly tone, "I hope you enjoyed the cookie-decorating class. My wife is a whiz with baked goods."

"Oh, it was a lot of fun," Chrissy said, the worry creasing her face beginning to soften. "I brought a cookie back for Wes, and he liked it. Nadine is a really good baker."

"Before she came to work here, she owned and ran a café in town. She was the pastry chef there for about ten years," he offered, taking a cursory glance around the suite. It had been decorated beautifully for the season, but unhappiness and tension hung in the air.

"What are you doing here, Sheriff?" Wes asked, his tone gruff and defensive.

"We have a warrant to search everyone's rooms and their belongings. Somebody staying at this bed-and-breakfast has to be the jewel thief."

The man's mouth formed a hard line. "And naturally you'd start with us."

Eli took the opportunity to sooth the man's ruffled feathers. "We have to start somewhere, Mr. Turner."

"Why us?" he challenged.

Chrissy placed a hand on her husband's back. "Why not us? Isn't it best to get it over with?"

Ignoring his wife's comment, Wes demanded, "Let me see your warrant."

Joe extended his phone for the man to see.

"That's your warrant? It doesn't look very official to me," Wes said after he'd studied it carefully.

"With road conditions being what they are, this is the best the judge could do. I assure you, it's legitimate. It gives us permission to search everything in your suite. It would be in your best interest to cooperate with us, Mr. Turner," Joe warned.

He snorted. "My best interest? Cooperating with law enforcement has never been in my best interest. You're just going to find a way to pin this on me."

The grandfather clock down the hall chimed eleven.

Joe softened his voice. "Your wife told us about your record, so I can understand why you'd feel that way. I assure you we're not trying to pin anything on you. We just have to figure out who committed this crime."

Wes turned a red face toward his wife. "You *told* them? How could you do that?"

Chrissy took a deep breath before responding. "So they know there's a reason you act the way you do and aren't just being a jerk."

With a huff, Wes finally agreed to the search. "Feel free to look around, gentlemen," he said, the words heavy with sarcasm. "I assure you that you won't find anything, but knock yourselves out." With that he turned and plopped down into an armchair to watch.

"You know, you don't have to be here for this," Eli reminded him.

Narrowing his eyes, Wes Turner growled, "You don't think I'm going to let you two rummage through our stuff unsupervised, do you?"

"I guess not. If you could stand up, I need to search that chair, then you're more than welcome to sit there and keep an eye on us," Eli offered.

"Fine," the grumpy man said, standing and taking a step off to the side to make room for the young deputy.

A couple of minutes later the chair had been thoroughly searched, Wes had reclaimed his seat, and the scowl that hadn't left his face was fixed firmly on Joe and Eli.

Doors and drawers squeaked open and banged shut for the next half hour. As Joe and Eli looked through the personal belongings of Wes and Chrissy Turner, they became more certain that though they'd looked the most suspicious, it was unlikely that the Turner couple had anything to do with the thefts.

Arms crossed over his chest in an aggressive and self-protecting posture, Wes's eyes never left the sheriff and his deputy.

"It looks like we're done here," Joe finally announced. "We didn't find anything."

"Of course you didn't. I told you we didn't take that jewelry." The arms were still crossed and his eyes still narrowed, but the ex-con's mouth had relaxed from an angry line into a frown.

"Thank you for your cooperation," Eli said in an appreciative tone. Wes Turner looked dangerous, and his previous attitude and behavior communicated that he was capable of violence.

"Not that I had a choice, but you're very welcome." Again, sarcasm laced the words. "I hope this means you'll be leaving us alone from now on."

"Unless you give us a reason to do otherwise, that's exactly what it means." Joe's words were clipped. He'd done his best to defuse the Turner man's bad attitude, but there was only so much he could take.

"Then consider this goodbye, because I have no intention of running into you again."

Joe and Eli gave a quick nod in Wes's direction, then turned toward Chrissy, who'd been reading quietly on the bed. "Ma'am, thank you for your cooperation," Joe said, sincerely this time. "I hope you'll take advantage of more of the festivities Marian has planned. I know the ladies have enjoyed getting to know you."

He was rewarded with a megawatt smile that left him wondering, What does a nice girl like that see in this guy?

He didn't have time to ponder his question, though. The jewelry was still missing, and he had more rooms to search.

Chapter Forty-Eight

"YOU'VE GOT TO get out of this room and live a little," Grant Hubley gently scolded. "I know that jewelry meant a lot to you, but you can't stay hidden away forever. The people here are very nice. They might just make you feel better."

Louise only frowned more. "Robbery makes a person feel so violated. I look around and wonder if there's anyone here I can trust. That makes me just want to stay in here by myself."

Professor Hubley shook his head and frowned. "The cookie-decorating class was a lot of fun, and I think you would have enjoyed the people there. Everyone seems genuinely nice. I think it would have been good for you. There's a Christmas card class in a little while. I think you should come. Learning how to decorate cookies and cards isn't exactly my thing, but it's a way to pass the time while we're stuck here."

She sighed. "I just don't know, Grant."

"You're being ridiculous," he finally said. "It's not like there's a murderer on the loose. No one's life is in danger here. Some jewelry was stolen, that's it."

"You know I've always been a little timid," Louise confessed. "This just has me shaken up."

The recently retired professor reached out and gently grasped his wife's shoulders. "I can understand that, Louise. I really can. Let's not start our new lives like this, though." He pulled her into an embrace.

Sinking into it, Louise breathed a little easier.

"What was that?" she asked after a moment.

"What was what?" Grant responded.

"That noise. Didn't you hear it?"

The two remained quiet for several moments until they heard the sound again. A thumping sound came from the room next door.

"Strange," Grant said, walking to the wall they shared with the Turner couple. Placing his ear against it, his brow furrowed as he listened. "Sounds like the sheriff and his deputy are in there searching the room. I wonder if they found the missing jewelry."

"Oh, Grant!" Louise cried. "Wouldn't it be wonderful if they recovered the things that were stolen?"

"Indeed it would," he responded. "Don't get your hopes up, though. You've been far too high-strung about this whole ordeal. It isn't good for your health. I'll go see if I can get some tea for you from the kitchen. Maybe that will help calm your nerves."

Louise nodded in agreement. "Thank you. That would be wonderful."

As her husband opened the door and disappeared, clicking

it shut behind him, Louise looked around the room. Despite the cheerful Christmas decor, she'd been chilled to the bone since last night. Under normal circumstances, the winking lights on the Christmas tree in the corner and the pine scent that wafted throughout the suite would have soothed her.

Not today, though. To say something was very wrong with this little trip Grant insisted they take was an understatement. Sometimes being married to an idealist was a real drag. He thought everything would always work out for them, never guessing that one day their luck might just run out.

Walking over to the fireplace, Louise flipped the switch that turned it on and watched as the flames leaped over the ceramic logs.

"If only it would warm me from the inside out," she muttered to herself, then thought gratefully of the tea her husband had gone to get for her. That should take care of the chill, she mused. Idealist though he may be, at least he was a thoughtful one.

She snagged the fleece bathrobe off the hook on the back of the bathroom door and wrapped it around herself, securely tying the belt to hold in as much heat as she could. Then, in preparation of the hot tea that would soon be coming, she sat in a chair near the fireplace and watched the flames dance. As the tension began to ease from her shoulders, a knock at the door pulled her out of the relaxed moment.

With a quick glance from side to side, not exactly sure what she was looking for, she stood and walked to the door.

"Who is it?" she called.

"Sheriff," the voice responded. "We have a warrant."

A chill raced down Louise's spine at the same time a knot

settled in the pit of her stomach. What do they want? she thought frantically. Grant was usually the one to deal with things like this.

Placing one clammy hand on the door knob, she opened the door and tried to smile. The surprised look on the faces of the sheriff and his deputy brought her full attention to the fact that she was still wearing a bathrobe.

"Good morning," she said, a bead of sweat popping up over her eyebrow. "Or is it afternoon? I didn't sleep much last night, so time is sort of running together."

"We understand," Joe said, then extended his phone in her direction. "We have a warrant to search each room in hopes of finding the missing jewelry."

"I hope chamomile is okay," Grant Hubley crowed as he walked into the room.

All eyes went to the professor.

"Oh, I wasn't aware we had company, or I would have brought something for you as well," he apologized as he handed the teacup and saucer to his wife. "As you can imagine, this theft has been hard on Louise. Is there anything I can help you with?"

Joe turned the screen of his phone toward Grant Hubley. "We have a warrant to search each of the rooms at the bed-and-breakfast. You're legally obligated to allow it, but it would be so much easier if you would also give us your permission. We've found there are fewer hard feelings that way."

"Of course," Mr. Hubley agreed. "We have nothing to hide."

"Glad to hear it," Joe said and meant it.

"Louise, dear, why don't we go to the sitting room and give these gentlemen some space. You can have your tea in front of the fire in there."

She placed her teacup and saucer on the small table next to the chair she'd just occupied and took off the bathrobe, draping over the back of the chair.

"You'll know where to find us if you have any questions," Mr. Hubley said. Then they were gone, leaving Joe and Eli to conduct their search.

An hour later, another search was complete, but they still hadn't found the jewelry.

"Strike two," Eli said, sounding as disappointed as Joe felt.

Joe nodded in agreement. "One more and we're out," he muttered.

The two men shared a pained glance. The next room to search was Cassandra Weaver's.

Chapter Forty-Nine

"M A'AM, YOU ARE compelled by law to let us search your room," Joe said, trying to keep his patience with Cassandra Weaver. "I have the search warrant right here."

Continuing to ignore the screen which held the emailed search warrant, Cassandra Weaver was becoming hysterical. "This is harassment!" she wailed.

"It's not," Eli countered, trying his hardest to sound sympathetic. "You reported that a piece of jewelry had been stolen, and it's our job to find it and make sure whoever stole it is brought to justice. But with all due respect, you're making it very difficult to do our job."

"Sure. Blame the victim." Her face was turning more red the angrier she became.

The two law enforcement officials shared a look of disbelief and discouragement. Neither had ever encountered someone this unhinged.

"Ma'am, no one is blaming you. We just need to look

around. For evidence." Joe's voice shook with the effort to stay calm.

"No."

"No?" Eli repeated. "What do you mean, 'no'? We have a warrant. You have to allow us to search your room."

"Let me get this straight," Joe began. "You reported a theft because you wanted your diamond chain back, and ever since then you've been the most uncooperative victim on the planet and refused to let us help you. Does that sound right?"

"You're not searching my room," Cassandra repeated emphatically.

"We are," Joe said in an even tone. "Even if we have to restrain you to do it."

"Restrain me?" the woman challenged. "Lay even a finger on me and I'll be screaming about police brutality to any news outlet that will listen."

"Unbelievable," Eli muttered.

Joe removed a pair of handcuffs from his belt. "Have it your way." In one quick movement, he had Cassandra Weaver's arms twisted behind her back and was snapping them on her wrists.

"I'll have your badge," she threatened.

"After dealing with the likes of you, you're welcome to it." Then turning to Eli, he said, "I'll do the search, you keep an eye on her and make sure she doesn't try anything."

"Sure thing," Eli agreed as he pushed down on the woman's shoulders, ensuring she'd have to sit down. Widening his stance, he crossed his arms in the most intimidating posture he could manage. Unfortunately, the woman didn't seem to notice.

As Joe opened the drawers of the dresser and night tables,

Cassandra hurled insults at him using every derogatory name in the book for police officers.

When he opened the door to the closet, he hit pay dirt.

"Well, well. What do we have here?" Joe said with a satisfied smile as he looked over at Cassandra. "How long did you think you could keep this up? Surely you had to have known we'd find out."

The hostile woman unexpectedly burst into tears, the sobs shaking her shoulders.

Joe jerked his head toward Eli, motioning his deputy to come see what he'd found.

Satisfied that the fight had gone out of the angry lady, Eli left his post and joined the sheriff.

"Take a look at that," Joe said, pointing to the closet floor.

"Well, I'll be." Eli turned to look once more at Cassandra Weaver, who looked like she wanted to shrink from existence. "Care to explain?"

She shook her head and stared down at the floor. "I want a lawyer," she said weakly.

Joe and Eli looked at each other. They'd have to honor her request, though how a lawyer could get to her on these roads was a mystery.

"Eli, please stand guard outside her room while I try to find a list of attorneys she could call."

The deputy nodded in agreement and followed him out into the hall.

"I guess that whole hysterical act was just to try to scare us out of searching her room," Joe observed.

"That lady does a good crazy person, that's for sure," Eli

said as he turned his back to the wall and cocked an ear in the direction of Cassandra's room.

"You said it," Joe agreed, then added, "You know, I'm beginning to hate Christmas."

Chapter Fifty

"KITTY LITTER?" MARIAN asked in disbelief when Joe filled her in on the developments in their case.

"You got it," Joe confirmed, then rubbed the stubble on his chin. The dark circles under his eyes told everyone present just how tired he was.

"Did you see a cat?" Nadine asked as she poured a cup of coffee, black, and pushed it toward her weary husband.

"I didn't see one, but there was a litter box and a bag of kitty litter in her closet. Unless she's using it herself, I guess there's a cat in there somewhere. It's good at hiding, I guess." He took a swallow of the coffee. "Thanks, Nay. I'm exhausted."

"You look like it."

"How's Josephine? I haven't seen her all day."

Nadine smiled. "She's great, as usual. Even got to visit with her two favorite aunts," she said, casting a glance at Holly and Sylvia. "They must have worn her out, because she's snoring like crazy during her nap."

Joe chuckled. "Let me see."

Nadine pulled her phone from her apron pocket and pulled up the video monitor they used to keep an eye on their daughter. Just as she'd said, Josephine was sleeping peacefully, a thumb in her mouth and snoring up a storm.

"As much as I love animals, guests aren't supposed to bring their pets," Marian said, clearly oblivious to the conversation between husband and wife.

"I think she knows that, which is why she did everything possible to keep us from searching her room. To be honest, she'd jumped right up to our number-one suspect for the jewel theft because of the way she was acting," Joe volunteered. "I've got Eli standing guard outside her room. Whether she was just acting like a crazy person or really is a little unhinged, I think it would be best to keep a close watch on her."

"Lucky him," Holly said dryly.

"He's a good deputy," Joe said. "He'll do what he has to do. Meanwhile, I need to come up with a list of attorneys Ms. Weaver can contact in the event that she needs one."

"An attorney?" Marian asked. "What would she need an attorney for?"

"In case legal action is taken against her for having a cat, I guess."

"That's ridiculous," the older woman said, waving her hand. "Why on earth would she think she'd need an attorney for breaking the pet policy at a local bed-and-breakfast?"

The tired sheriff took another drink of coffee and shrugged. "Beats me. There's something off about her."

"Didn't we say yesterday before dinner that she seemed like a cat lady?" Nadine said to Marian.

"Yes, and didn't I say I hoped she didn't have one stashed away in her room?" Marian answered. "As much as I don't want the place smelling like cat pee, I'm not the kind of person who would press charges because somebody took their cat on vacation."

"But she doesn't know that," Nadine pointed out, then slid her arm around Marian's shoulders. "We all know you have the patience of a saint and a heart of gold, but she doesn't."

"Maybe I should go talk to her," Marian suggested.

"I don't know if that's a good idea," Joe warned. "Like I said, she's not quite right."

"Nonsense," Marian said, dismissing Joe's concern. "She won't try to hurt me. Besides, Eli will be right there if I need him."

"Suit yourself," Joe grudgingly acquiesced. "I hope you'll have better luck with her than we have."

"While you're doing that, Marian, I need to get things ready for our next class," Ivy said from the corner of the kitchen where she'd been listening to the talk about Cassandra-the-cat-lady.

"I'll help," Holly volunteered. "But the rest of you need to clear out."

The rest of the group obediently filed out of the kitchen—Marian to have a chat with Ms. Weaver, Joe to compile a list of attorneys, and the others to do who knows what.

As Holly and Ivy quietly got the supplies ready for the Christmas card-making class, a tension filled the air that spoke not of the end of the trouble at the Farmhouse Inn, but that there was more trouble to come.

Chapter Fifty-One

MARIAN JINGLED DOWN the hallway as the bells around the hem of her elf costume and on the toes of her shoes swayed back and forth with each movement. She nodded at Eli when she got to Cassandra Weaver's door.

Eli's eyes narrowed when he saw her. "What are you doing here?"

"Besides the fact that I own the place?" Marian teased with a wink, then lowered her voice. With a wave of her hand in the direction of Cassandra's door, she said, "I need to talk to her. It would seem like she's blowing things way out of proportion."

"That's an understatement. I've never seen anybody act the way she has," Eli confided.

"So I've heard. I'm going to try to get to the bottom of things and make her realize that smuggling a cat in here isn't a criminal offense." Marian almost chuckled at the ridiculousness of the idea.

Eli didn't see the humor in it. "We already tried that. The woman isn't right. I don't think you should go in there."

Marian patted his arm. "That's why you're here," she reminded him, then raised her hand to knock on the door.

"Who is it now?" a watery and anguished voice asked from inside the room.

A wave of compassion washed over Marian. Her guest was clearly upset, and she'd do whatever she could to fix it. "Marian Bright," she responded. "I want to talk to you for a minute."

The door swung open, and a tear-stained Cassandra Weaver stood in front of Marian, clutching a black cat to her chest.

"May I come in?" Marian asked.

Cassandra shrugged. "It's your place. You can do whatever you want." Her eyes cut toward Eli, whose mouth dipped into a frown, though he said nothing.

Marian stepped forward into the woman's room and closed the door, leaving the deputy out in the hall. "May I?" she asked, motioning to one of the chairs by the cheerfully decorated fireplace.

"Go ahead," Cassandra agreed as she settled into the one opposite the geriatric elf.

"I hear we've had a little trouble," Marian began, slipping into the grandmotherly role she was so good at.

Ms. Weaver shrugged and snuggled her cat closer, saying nothing.

"Can we talk about it?"

Looking up with tears rimming her eyes, Cassandra begged, "Please don't take her from me. She's all I have left in the world."

Marian's compassion for the woman grew. "I have no intention of taking her from you. Why don't you tell me a little bit about what's going on." She reached out to pet the cat, who immediately started purring.

"Her name is Onyx. She likes you." The woman sighed, then began speaking. "I needed to get away. I just left an abusive relationship, and I wanted to go somewhere remote where he couldn't contact me," she said as she stroked the cat's head.

"That was very brave of you."

A small smile tugged at Cassandra's mouth. "Thanks, but I don't feel very brave."

"Tell me about Onyx," Marian nudged, hoping the change in topic would make the woman open up.

"I rescued her when she was just a kitten. She was so tiny, I had to feed her with an eyedropper. The vet said her chance of survival was really low because she was so tiny and weak. I made it my mission to make sure she survived. Now she's my best friend. Please don't take her away from me," Cassandra begged again, her voice thick with tears.

Marian scooted the chair closer to Cassandra and her cat. "I already told you I have no intention of taking your cat. Can you tell me why you've asked for a lawyer?"

Straightening her spine, Cassandra said, "To protect us. They won't let me have a cat if I'm in jail."

Furrowing her brows, Marian asked, "Why would you go to jail?"

Disbelief sprang onto the woman's face. "Because I brought a cat, and you have a no-pet policy."

Marian smirked. This woman surely didn't have a clear idea of how the world worked. "Dear, breaking the pet policy of a bed-and-breakfast is hardly punishable by law. The one thing you *don't* have to worry about is anyone pressing charges against you because you brought your cat. The worst that would happen would be that I charged you an extra cleaning fee, which I'm not inclined to do."

"No?"

"Of course not. It's Christmas, for Pete's sake! It would take Scrooge himself to punish someone for taking their best friend on vacation at Christmas, and the one thing I'm not is Scrooge."

For the first time since Marian first met her, Cassandra's face lightened, and a look of peace came over her. "So I don't need a lawyer, after all?"

Marian reached over and gave the woman's hand a squeeze. "No, dear. You don't need a lawyer, but it would be helpful if you'd cooperate with Sheriff Adler and Deputy Nolan. They still have a crime to solve."

Cassandra hugged her cat so close that Marian was sure the poor thing would suffocate. "I'll cooperate," she said, loosening her grasp on the cat.

With a final smile, Marian stood and walked to the door. "They'll treat you well. I'm sure of it." She twisted the doorknob and pulled it open. "She's all yours," she told the dumbfounded deputy.

"You have actual magic powers, don't you?" he asked.

She shook her head and grinned. "It's not magic, it's Christmas."

Chapter Fifty-Two

A FEW MINUTES LATER, Marian had retrieved Joe and he was in Cassandra's room with Eli, waiting for her to tell them everything she could about the theft.

"So the diamond chain was actually a collar for Onyx," the woman confessed.

A puzzled frown crept between Joe's eyebrows. "The diamonds were for a *cat*? Where they real diamonds?"

"Of course they were real. Only the best for Ms. Kitty," she said in a tone that communicated putting diamonds on a cat was the most natural thing in the world.

"My wife doesn't even have diamonds," Joe grumbled.

"Mine either," Eli commiserated.

Cassandra shrugged. "She's all I have. She saved me."

Joe rubbed his forehead. "So we're looking for a diamond cat collar? Can you give us a more detailed description than that?" the sheriff asked, visibly miffed that the precious stones that were missing belonged to a feline.

"I can do better than that," the woman said as she reached

for her phone. She pulled up the photos she'd taken and scrolled until she found one that was a close-up of Onyx wearing a collar that sparkled in the light shining overhead.

"Nice bling," Eli said wryly. Any normal human would think putting diamonds on a creature that licked itself would be a tad much. This woman had shown them that she certainly wasn't a normal human.

"Would you like a copy of the picture?"

"Uh, I think we'll be okay," Joe said.

Cassandra looked troubled. "How will you know if you've found the right thing?"

Joe's mouth twisted into a smirk. "How about this? We'll have you check out any diamond cat collars we come across."

That seemed to satisfy the woman.

Once the two men were outside her room, they looked at each other. "Can you believe that?" Joe said, hooking his thumb over his shoulder.

"She lives in a totally different world than the rest of us, but I think we already knew that," Eli observed.

They let silence float between them for a moment before Joe said, "Strike three."

Eli suddenly looked somber. "Looks like we're out."

After coming up empty in each of the guest suites, the sheriff and his deputy began the tedious task of searching each nook and cranny in every other room in the house. It was a slow, irritating process that tested the limits of both men's patience.

So far, they'd checked everywhere in the sitting room,

dining room, and had emptied each drawer and cabinet in the kitchen in the search for the missing jewelry. Ivy, a frown marring her otherwise girl-next-door face, stood nearby, supervising the destruction of the heart of the home.

"Nothing," Eli announced as he stood from the low cabinet he'd been searching.

"Here either," Joe said as he snapped a drawer in the island shut. "Where could that stuff be? We've searched everywhere."

Eli chewed his lip in thoughtful silence before speaking. "Not everywhere."

"What's left?" the sheriff asked, exasperated.

The deputy raised a shoulder and let it drop. "Our stuff."

"*Our* stuff? We didn't take it," Joe countered.

"I don't just mean yours and mine. I mean the locals. We haven't searched their stuff yet."

"That's ridiculous," Joe muttered, but deep down he knew Eli was right. It was their duty to check every possibility.

"Does the warrant cover them?"

Joe nodded. "If they're in this house, it covers them."

"This should be easy since none of us brought anything with us except our jackets, gloves, and scarves. Plus, handbags for the ladies."

They began by gathering all the Saddle Hill residents into a group and leaving them sitting by the fireplace with glasses of eggnog that Marian had graciously poured.

Beginning with the jackets hanging by the back door in the kitchen, the two men rummaged through each pocket. They pulled gloves out of the pockets and felt inside each one. When they'd reached the last jacket, Joe plunged his hand into the pocket and froze.

Surely not, he thought.

Grabbing hold of the contents of the pocket, he withdrew his hand. When he released his fist, a diamond collar was winking up at him, along with a pair of earrings and a necklace.

"I found them," Joe said glumly, wishing he hadn't.

Eli turned to look at him, the color draining from his face. "Where did you find them?" he asked warily.

Joe pointed to a black jacket with a multicolored knit scarf around the neck. "In one of the pockets of that jacket."

The tip of Eli's tongue poked out to lick his lips. He swallowed hard. It took a minute for him to find his words. In a hoarse voice, Eli finally said, "That's Holly's jacket."

Chapter Fifty-Three

"WHAT DO YOU mean the missing jewelry was found in my coat pocket?" Holly asked as she shot to her feet. Her eyes darted around the room. "That's impossible. I didn't take anything."

The room fell silent, the eyes of all the Saddle Hill residents resting on her. Some looked too shocked to speak, others were vehemently shaking their heads, unable to believe Holly would do such a thing.

Joe looked so distraught he might has well have delivered a terminal diagnosis to his best friend, and Eli looked like he could throw up.

"That's preposterous," Ralph finally said, breaking the silence. "Holly has worked in my store for more than two years. If she was going to steal something, wouldn't she have already done it?"

"I've told you all, that part of my life is behind me!" Holly insisted. "I haven't stolen anything since I came to Saddle Hill. Why would I risk the life I've built? Especially now that I'm married to a man in law enforcement?"

Marian, who'd been sitting next to Holly on the sofa, grasped the young woman's hand and pulled her back to her seat. "No one can truly believe that you'd do such a thing, dear," the grandmotherly woman assured her.

"There's no way you could have taken that jewelry. You were with us," Sylvia spoke up.

"That's true," Nadine agreed. "When Mrs. Hubley's jewelry went missing, you were sitting at the table with everybody else. You have an alibi."

"What about Ms. Weaver's diamond chain?" Kris asked. "Does anybody actually know when that was taken?"

The sheriff shook his head. "She said she noticed it was missing this morning before breakfast."

"And she hadn't looked for it until then?" James Jingle clarified, following the lead of his son.

"No," Eli said quietly, still looking pale.

"I think we can all agree that Holly wouldn't have stolen those things," Carla said, inserting herself into the conversation.

"And we all know that it's not hard to frame somebody for jewel theft," Kris reminisced. It didn't seem like that long ago that he was sitting behind bars because somebody did the same thing to him. "But Joe, you and Marian solved that one, and I'm sure we're all confident that you can solve this one, too."

A half dozen heads nodded in agreement.

"Marian, why don't you, Joe, and Eli put your heads together to figure out what's going on around here and how that jewelry found its way into Holly's coat. Ivy and I will take care of everything in the kitchen," Nadine volunteered.

The members of the group reluctantly stood, looking to each other for some kind of guidance about what to do next.

Holly, who looked as though somebody had knocked the wind out of her, was still seated on the sofa. "What do I do?" she asked, almost numbly.

Marian patted her hand. "Why don't you stay with Nadine and Ivy. I'm sure they could use your help." She looked at Sylvia. "Will you help them, too?"

"Of course," Sylvia agreed. She took Holly's hand from Marian and guided her to the kitchen. "I'll get you a hot cup of tea. That will help soothe you."

Holly, like an obedient child, followed her friend to the kitchen.

"Joe, Eli, and I will need some time to sort things out," Marian said to Ralph and Carla Stockton, as well as James, Patricia, and Kris Jingle. "Keep your ears to the ground and see what you can find out from the victims. You can use the phone in the dining room to call their rooms. All the numbers to the individual rooms are taped to the underside of the phone. Invite them out for hot chocolate and a game, or even to make the Christmas cards we never got around to. Obviously we're behind schedule with our activities due to the interviews and room searches. Just do what you can to get everyone out of their rooms. We need to know what they know."

"Yes, ma'am," James said heartily.

"Good luck," Carla and Patricia said in unison.

"You've figured this stuff out before. You can do it again," Ralph said, cheering on the trio of crime-fighters.

"I'll do what I can," Kris promised.

With the marching orders given, Marian, Joe, and Eli left the others in the sitting room and went to her office and closed the door. They'd solved a case of jewelry theft before, but this almost seemed harder with no access to outside resources.

The irony that didn't escape Marian is that two of the suspects from that case were here at the bed-and-breakfast. They'd found Ralph Stockton's Christmas star in Kris's employee locker at the mall where he worked as a Santa. It had taken Marian and Joe's tireless efforts to find the real thief, who turned out to be Kris's brother. The previous sheriff had been no help, since he was only interested in having someone behind bars so he could move on to bigger and better things.

The last they'd heard, though, the previous sheriff was unable to find the kind of job he wanted and thought he deserved and was working as a security guard in a mall in some big city.

Holly was suspected of stealing the star only because she was new in town and had previously admitted to Marian that she had a police record for theft. When she went missing, it was only natural to wonder if she'd stolen the star and split. It was only later that Holly was found locked in a janitorial closet in Whipple's Wicks and was able to tell the story about what really happened: she'd been locked in the closet by Ralph Stockton's bitter and materialistic wife—the wife who, in an unexpected twist of fate was later arrested for stealing valuable jewelry from Ralph's store throughout their two-year marriage.

The motivation for everyone's task was evident: clear Holly's name and bring the real thief to justice.

Chapter Fifty-Four

SYLVIA, NADINE, AND Ivy bustled around the kitchen as Holly sat, still as stone, in a chair at the kitchen counter. The festivity of the holiday was obviously doing nothing to cheer her. Not even the holly arrangement in the center island, full and covered in bright red berries.

"It's like my worst nightmare has come true," she moaned miserably as Sylvia slid a cup of hot tea in front of her. "I didn't steal that jewelry."

"We know that," Nadine assured her and slid a plate holding a leftover biscuit from breakfast in front of her. "Nobody thinks you actually took it."

Holly raised the teacup to her lips and took a huge gulp, then sputtered as she spit it back out. "That's hot."

Without saying a word, Ivy grabbed a dish towel and mopped up the mess on the counter. "Let it cool a bit," she suggested, then offered, "Or if you want to drink it right away, I can get you an ice cube."

"That's very nice of you," Holly said, her voice still sounding detached. "I'll be okay, though. Really."

Ivy nodded and took the towel over to a small basket they used for dirty towels and dishcloths in the corner by the back door and dropped it in. Turning back to the small group of ladies, she asked, "Who else would have had access to the kitchen besides us? Pretty much just the people that live around here. I don't think the kitchen has been left unattended all day."

Nadine and Sylvia frowned. "You're probably right. At least one of us has been in here practically all day," Nadine confirmed.

"But somebody could make the argument that I could have slipped it into my coat pocket when I was alone in here," Holly pointed out.

Sylvia placed her hands on her hips. "But who would say that?" she challenged. "None of us think you did it, the Jingles and Stocktons don't think you did it, Joe doesn't seem to think so and I know Eli doesn't think you did. Who's left to accuse you?"

"The victims. When they find out their jewelry was found in *my* coat pocket, they'll be out for blood. My blood," Holly moaned.

"Well, first of all," Sylvia began. "I don't think any of them would try to hurt you. Second, how would they know the jewelry was found with your stuff?"

Holly nervously picked at her fingernails. "When the guys tell them they recovered their jewelry, won't they ask who took it?"

Nadine and Sylvia looked at each other. She had a point.

"Well, I'm sure Joe and Eli would keep your name out of it. The last thing they'd want to do is draw a target on your back when we're all stuck here together with no way to escape until the roads are clear," Nadine replied.

As the women thought it over, the back door opened and a gust of frigid air whooshed in.

"What's with the sour faces?" Vito asked as he looked from one woman to the next.

All eyes went to Holly as they tried to decide how to respond.

Holly covered her face with her hands. "It's fine. You can tell him. Vito's been on the wrong side of the law, too. He'll understand."

Vito's eyebrows shot up and he pulled the knit cap off his head. "What's going on?" he whispered to Sylvia.

She lowered her voice to match his. "They found the missing jewelry in Holly's coat pocket."

"You're kidding." From his tone of voice, it was clear he didn't believe it either.

Shaking her head tightly, Sylvia said, "They did. Of course, none of us believe she actually stole it."

Vito crossed the kitchen in a few long strides and stopped next to Holly. "I'm so sorry. Does anybody have any idea how it got there?"

Her face still buried in her hands, a sob escaped from Holly's throat. Her dazed facade finally cracking, she wailed, "No! Everyone is going to think I did it since I have a record."

With a comforting hand on her shoulder, Vito said gently, "I highly doubt anybody that knows you will think you stole those things. It doesn't matter if you have a record, that doesn't mean you can't turn your life around." He smiled and spread his arms wide. "Look at me. I kidnapped the spirit of Christmas last year, and here I am making an honest living."

Holly's sobs subsided and were reduced to sniffles. "Thank you."

With a quick tilt of his head, he acknowledged her thanks and turned to come face-to-face with Sylvia, who was smiling in admiration.

"Thank you," she said. "I think you made her feel better than the rest of us could, combined."

"Anytime," Vito replied. "Now all we have to do is find out who put the jewelry in her pocket."

Chapter Fifty-Five

RALPH HUNG UP the phone and turned to the others. "I think the Turners are going to come. The husband didn't sound too keen on it, but the wife was excited."

"Great!" Patricia said enthusiastically. "She seems really nice. Despite the fact that her husband is about as anti-social as they come, I like her."

"Next up, the Hubleys," Ralph remarked as he lifted the receiver and punched in the number that would connect him with Grant and Louise Hubley's room.

"I sure hope Louise will come out of her room," Carla commented as her husband waited to be connected with the couple. "It's not good for a person to be alone in times of trouble."

James Jingle nodded. "I couldn't agree more. When we thought Kris stole Ralph's star, and when it turned out Nicholas was the one who did it and framed Kris, we—particularly me— were too embarrassed to be around other people. I thought I'd be judged for how my kids turned out. Because of that, I took away the opportunity for our friends to help us."

"And I've always been a loner," Kris added. "That's mostly because I always felt different from everybody else. If I could go back and change things, I'd be more open to allowing others to get to know me. I'd probably have better social skills if I did." Kris chuckled at his own joke.

His parents laughed as well. "If you had, maybe you wouldn't have fallen for that Carol Ling person last year. She was a piece of work, that one," his mother pointed out.

Heat prickled the back of Kris's neck. His relationship with the reporter who ended up just using him to get information in order to help her career wasn't his finest moment.

"I knew it was too good to be true," he said wryly. "I'm sure I'm not the first one to be taken in by a pretty face."

"No, son, you certainly aren't," his father affirmed.

The click of the phone brought the conversation to a standstill.

"Are they in?" Carla asked her husband.

Ralph nodded. "Grant is, for sure. He said he'd do his best with Louise." He shrugged. "She's a strange lady. Seems scared of her own shadow."

"Speaking of strange lady," Kris interjected. "I guess Cassandra Weaver is the last one to call."

With a visible shudder, Ralph asked, "Does somebody want to relieve me of that duty?" He looked into the blank faces of his wife and friends. "Nobody, really? I braved the possibility of angering Wes Turner. The least one of you can do is volunteer to take care of this call."

"It should probably be a woman, considering the fact that she's single and it seems like she doesn't trust men," James pointed out.

Patricia scowled. "So that would leave me or Carla. How do we decide? I doubt either of us are going to jump at the chance."

"Rock, paper, scissors?" Kris asked, suggesting the time-honored tradition of decision-making when no one wanted to do the job.

"Fine," Carla agreed. "Loser has to call her?"

Patricia nodded and the two women got in the ready position.

Cries of "ooohhh" rang out from the small crowd when the peeved former Mrs. Claus saw that Carla's rock crushed her scissors.

Patricia sighed deeply. "Give me the phone," she demanded, then pushed the buttons to be connected to the Weaver woman's room.

The group watched intently as Patricia gave the invitation and then listened for the answer. After hanging up the receiver, she turned to face the group head-on.

"Well, is she coming?" James asked impatiently when Patricia didn't speak right away.

Patricia nodded. "She said she would. She sounded a little down but was perfectly nice."

"Good!" James enthused. "Let's get some games out and get ready to play."

"I'll go to the kitchen for eggnog," Carla said, then added, with a wink, "And maybe some rum after the way the weekend has turned out so far."

❧

Fifteen minutes later, the Saddle Hill residents, as well as the inn's paying guests, were seated at the table in the dining room. Nadine's centerpiece of greenery, battery-operated candles, pine cones, and poinsettias had been removed and the center of the table now held two different board games. Wes, Chrissy, and the Jingle crew opted for Clue, while the Stocktons, Hubleys, and Cassandra settled in for a long game of Monopoly, Saddle Hill edition.

Soon, eggnog was poured—some with rum, some without—and the group was chatting like old friends. Even Wes Turner had started to loosen up and seemed to be enjoying himself. Louise Hubley acted a little more confident and less the delicate wallflower than she had been before.

Though the quintet learned interesting things about their guests, none of them knew what was important and what wasn't. A debriefing with the sheriff, his deputy, and Saddle Hill's number-one crime-solving elf would be required to find out if anything important had been said.

Nadine came into the dining room carrying a tray of brownies.

With a smile, Chrissy plucked one from the platter and announced, "We're all going to be nice and plump after this visit."

Ralph and James looked down at their already-round mid-sections. "Just what we need," Ralph said wryly.

Everyone at the table laughed together, and Nadine smiled. The Saddle Hill crew had done the impossible.

They'd built a friendship with the guests. One of whom was a thief.

Chapter Fifty-Six

"HOW DID IT go?" Marian asked cautiously when she, Joe, and Eli came out of their meeting.

"It was great," Carla volunteered. "We've got some fun folks staying here."

"You'd never know it by the way things started off, but we loosened them up," James added.

A smile spread across Marian's face. "How did you manage that? They were as grumpy as can be earlier."

"Just by being our typical friendly and charming selves," Ralph joked, then became serious. "Cassandra said you were the reason she felt better, Marian. She said you were so kind to her and put her mind at ease, so she was finally able to let go and have fun. Since her secret is out, I suppose she decided there was nothing else to lose. She's strange, but once she loosened up, she was fun to have around."

"A Christmas miracle," Joe said wryly. "After the way she treated me and Eli, I thought the woman didn't have a decent bone in her body."

Marian, still donning her elf costume, shook her head. "That just goes to show you how heavy carrying around a secret can be. Lies just pile up and become a burden no one can carry. It could turn anyone into a grump. Ms. Weaver is also an example of how a little kindness can make all the difference in the world. She told me some of her story, and it turns out she's a pretty brave woman."

Carla and Patricia busied themselves replacing the table decorations, while the others continued talking.

"It's funny, though, none of the robbery victims wanted to play Clue," Kris said, deep in thought. "It was almost as though they wanted to distance themselves from any kind of crime, even a fictional one."

"That could be nothing," Ralph countered with a shrug. "Professor Hubley told me he'd considered going into real estate in his retirement. That could be why he wanted to play Monopoly."

"Can you even imagine Louise in real estate? She has the personality of a wet mop. I can't see her being able to sell anything," Patricia added.

"Did you get a whiff of her?" Carla asked as she straightened the greens running down the length of the table. "She smelled like she'd dumped a whole bottle of baby powder on herself."

Patricia, nestling the pine cones into their spots in the greens, said, "Maybe she's got social anxiety that makes her sweaty and the baby powder will help absorb that."

"Funny," Eli said. "We found a giant bottle of baby powder in the Hubleys' bathroom when we were searching their room. I wondered if they had a baby stashed in their room somewhere. Josephine isn't missing any powder, is she?"

Joe shrugged. "I have no idea. I haven't even seen my own daughter since this began."

As if on cue, Nadine came in the dining room from the kitchen. She glanced towards Joe, Marian, and Eli. "How's it going?" she asked.

"Fine," Eli replied. "We were just asking Joe if Josephine was missing any baby powder."

"Baby powder?"

Marian nodded. "It would seem that Louise Hubley has an affinity for baby powder."

"Weird." Nadine's mouth twisted in confusion.

"Eh, it's probably nothing," Carla said, taking a step back from the table and admiring her work with the greens. "Forget I said anything."

Despite Carla's disregard for Louise's partiality for baby powder, something kept bugging Marian. She watched the battery-operated candles flicker on the table.

What was it that kept nagging her?

Chapter Fifty-Seven

HOLLY WAS STILL despondent in the kitchen when Marian entered. Sylvia comforted her friend the best she could, but Holly didn't respond.

When Marian entered the room, Sylvia straightened up, removing her arm from around her young friend's shoulders. "Well? Did you figure anything out?" she demanded.

Marian's eyes moved to the woman who'd become like a granddaughter to her. Holly's long red hair was tousled, the spray of freckles across her nose dark against her pale face. Compassion filled the older woman's heart. "Oh, Holly. Is there anything I can do to help?"

Holly shrugged and slowly raised her eyes to meet Marian's. "Find out who is trying to frame me." Her voice was monotone and unfeeling.

To Marian, it seemed as though Holly was looking at her but not really seeing her. "We will," Marian promised. "Did you see or hear anything that might give us a clue as to who might have had the opportunity to slip in here and put the jewelry in your pocket?"

Shaking her head numbly, she muttered, "I have no idea who would do such a thing."

"On the bright side," Sylvia interjected, "it seems like framing you wasn't necessarily intentional. What I mean is, they weren't targeting you specifically. Other than those of us who know you, how could the others possibly know what jacket was yours? My guess is that it provided an opportunity for the real thief to not get caught. Nothing more."

Marian's eyes sparkled as the realization sunk in. "That's right! Somebody needed to dispose of the jewelry, and fast. Why would they be in such a rush?"

Holly and Sylvia just watched Marian, waiting for her to answer her own question.

"Because they knew the rooms were being thoroughly searched, that's why!" Marian shouted triumphantly. "Now we just need to gather everyone together and ask if anybody saw someone that had the opportunity to go in the kitchen. I think they're still in the dining room."

As the ladies filed out of the kitchen, they looked at all the residents of Saddle Hill that were still gathered. Though none of them were perfect, they'd become family. Surely one of them would know something that would help Holly.

⸙

Twenty minutes later, they all realized none of them knew who could have had an opportunity to slip the jewelry into Holly's coat pocket.

"I'm so sorry," Ralph said as he patted Holly's knee. "There's nothing we'd like more than to be able to get to the bottom of this."

Nodding, tears seeped out of Holly's eyes. "This is such a nightmare," she moaned.

Kris spoke up. "Can I just say what we're all thinking? Charges haven't been pressed against you, Holly. Nobody believes you did it, and nobody is looking at you like you're a crook. Can you please pull it together? I understand you have a past, but nobody believes you're still stealing things. Yet, here you are, being all weepy and moping around like handcuffs are about to descend from the heavens and shackle themselves around your wrists. It's just not true, so cut it out. If you'd pull yourself out of this pity party, you might actually have something to contribute." Sinking back in his chair, he crossed his arms across his chest and waited for someone to yell at him. There were plenty of mouths hanging open, but so far no one had spoken.

"Now, you wait just a minute," Eli said, anger burning in his eyes. "Don't you dare talk to my wife like that."

Holly sniffed and shook her head. "No, Kris is right. I'm so worried about how everyone is viewing me that I've been no help at all." She turned toward the youngest Jingle present. "Thank you. I needed that kick in the pants."

"Do you remember anyone going into the kitchen?" James Jingle asked.

Holly's face scrunched in thought. "Not that I remember. That doesn't mean anything, though. I'll take some time to think about it, and maybe I'll come up with something."

"Think about it while we make dinner," Marian ordered. "We're having lasagna tonight and need to get it going."

As the group dispersed, an image tickled Holly's memory, but she couldn't quite pull it to the front of her mind.

It'll come to me, she thought as she followed Marian and Sylvia back to the kitchen to start the dinner preparations.

Chapter Fifty-Eight

CASSANDRA HUGGED HER cat tightly against her chest as tears of joy ran down her cheeks, soaking the jet-black fur.

"Our secret is out, darling, and it's okay," she whispered with relief. "They won't be taking you away from me."

Marian wasn't going to take Onyx away and press charges against her. She clearly wasn't thrilled that her "No Pets" policy had been broken, but she was understanding and compassionate when Cassandra told her about the reason she needed the cat with her.

For years she'd been at the mercy of an abusive husband. Time after time, she'd ended up in the emergency room with "unexplained" injuries. One day she'd decided enough was enough and she gathered all her courage and walked out, fully expecting that he'd come after her.

Maybe he had—she didn't know.

Not staying in one place for very long, she'd been able to stay off his radar. When the ice storm hit last night, she was both relieved and terrified. With the roads the way they are, he'd never be able to get to her, but on the other hand, if he found a way, she wouldn't been able to get away.

Despite the fact that she'd given Sheriff Adler and Deputy Nolan a hard time and was as uncooperative as she could be, she was actually glad they were there. Just knowing law enforcement was around made her feel a little safer.

She stroked Onyx's head. "It's all going to be okay now."

And it will, she reminded herself.

Dinner would be served soon, and when it was, she would be at the table, ready to apologize for causing the sheriff and his deputy so much trouble. She'd talk to the others and actually enjoy her evening. Whether she got Onyx's diamond collar back or not, it really wasn't important. What was important was that she had her best friend, and she was safe—something she hadn't felt for a very long time.

Chapter Fifty-Nine

THE CONVERSATION AROUND the dinner table was much more amicable than it had been the night before. The ice stopped coming down earlier in the afternoon, and the sun had been shining on the coated blades of grass with the benefit of both beginning to melt it and make it shine like millions of diamonds.

The guests had even begun to murmur that maybe they'd be able to leave soon, though it didn't seem as though anyone was as eager to leave as they had been.

Now dusk, the ice diamonds no longer glistened and there was the fear that in the dark of night, everything that had melted would refreeze and make conditions even worse.

Despite that possibility, tonight there was laughter and community that had been missing among the guests before.

Even Cassandra, now unafraid about her secret being found out, even showed a charming side of her personality that nobody had known was there. "This lasagna is delicious," she commented as she shoveled a large forkful into her mouth. "It's always been my favorite."

Remarks such as "the best I've ever had" and "this is the best comfort food for a winter night" were murmured, much to Marian's delight.

"My Roger used to love this meal." Her face took on a wistful, faraway look. "I've tried to have all his favorites on rotation for dinners. Sometimes, when I'm dishing up his favorites, it feels like he's still here."

"Who's Roger?" Chrissy Turner asked.

"My late husband," Marian explained. "He passed nearly three years ago."

"I'm sorry," the young woman said, and looked like she really meant it.

"Thank you, dear. They say time heals all wounds, but I say that time just brings a new normal," Marian said wisely. "I imagine that's the case with all life-changing events. We never really get over them, but we learn how to live with them."

Chrissy reached over to her husband and ran the backs of her fingers down his cheek. "I guess that's all we can do," she murmured, her eyes never leaving his face.

"That's pretty wise," Wes commented, then reached up and grasped his wife's hand in his own. "That's something I'd do well to remember."

Mrs. Turner beamed at her husband as though there had been an unexpected change in him.

"If you think the lasagna was good," Ivy commented as she cleared the plates from the table, "wait until you try her brownie sundaes."

"Can't wait," a chorus of voices exclaimed.

Several minutes later, each person at the table sat behind a bowl with a giant brownie and a huge scoop of ice cream. Small pitchers of dessert sauces, as well as bowls with crushed candy and nuts, completed the spread. As each bowl and pitcher was passed around, the dessert mounds got higher and higher. As the first bites were taken, the exclamations of pure joy made Marian's heart swell. Brownie sundaes had been Roger's favorite dessert. Somehow, she knew he was approving of her menu choice for the evening.

Marian's reminiscing was interrupted by Cassandra Weaver, who'd begun to tell a story about a time when she was baking brownies. "And there was my cat, Onyx, with her face in the bag of flour. Even though I dusted her off, I couldn't get all the flour out of her fur. Poor thing. With the flour in her black fur, she ended up looking like an old, gray cat." Ms. Weaver took another bite of her dessert.

Slowly, Cassandra's words sunk in. A powder would make dark hair look gray. As the pieces of the puzzle fell into place, Marian was overcome with the certainty that she knew who the jewel thief was.

Chapter Sixty

WHEN THE TABLE was finally cleared, Marian motioned for Joe and Eli to follow her to her office. "I know what happened," she said urgently once she'd closed the door behind them.

Their eyebrows shot up. "You *know* who the thief is?" Joe asked impatiently. "Who?"

Marian looked around as though someone could be eavesdropping, then hissed, "The Hubleys."

"The Hubleys? But they were one of the victims," Eli disagreed.

"Unless they weren't," Marian countered, then turned her attention to Joe. "You remember our list of suspects for Ralph's star a couple years ago. Who was on that list even though he was a victim?"

"Ralph," Joe said firmly, picking up on Marian's logic.

"Exactly! What if the Hubleys were the first 'victims' so they could remove themselves from suspicion? What if Onyx's diamond collar was the target the whole time?"

At that, Joe looked skeptical. "How would they possibly know about it? They never met until they were here together. Besides, she didn't exactly broadcast that she'd smuggled a cat in here. You saw the way she acted to keep anybody from finding out."

Nodding her head in agreement, Marian replied, "I know. So they had to have found out another way."

Eli shook his head. "I don't know…"

"I do." Marian's chin lifted in defiance of their skepticism. "All we need to do now is prove it."

"How, exactly, do you suggest we do that?" Joe challenged.

Marian placed a finger on her chin. "Give me a minute to think."

While Marian devised a plan to prove that the retired professor and his awkward wife were the thieves, Holly busted through the door.

"I know who was in the kitchen!" Holly exclaimed. "I was too wrapped up in myself to remember before, but now I know!"

Marian shushed her and gestured for Holly to lower her voice. "Who?"

"Grant Hubley," Holly disclosed. "I remember I was in the kitchen talking to Sylvia. We were having a serious conversation, so I barely noticed, but Grant Hubley came into the kitchen for some tea for his wife. Ivy got it for him, so I never paid him any mind."

"Interesting," Joe muttered. "Do you remember if he was over by the coat rack?"

Holly shook her head. "I don't. I'm sorry. Like I said, Sylvia and I were deep in conversation."

"If that's the case, and he knew they weren't paying attention to him, he could have slipped it in Holly's coat pocket while Ivy was busy pouring the tea," Marian suggested.

Joe's eyes narrowed as he considered the possibility. "He had opportunity."

"Maybe he wanted to make sure nobody found it during the search," Holly theorized.

Eli slowly nodded his head, but said, "How would he have known we were doing the search right then? He would have had to find out about it somehow."

"Maybe he heard you through the wall. They share a wall with the Turners. If they heard you searching their room, they could have known."

"Grant did come back with the tea when we were already in their room," Eli offered.

"See? It had to be him," Holly pressed.

Joe's mouth dipped into a frown. "But how will we prove it?"

"Isn't the timing and an eyewitness enough proof?" Holly demanded. "I saw him!"

"I'm afraid not," Eli said gently. "That would be circumstantial evidence at best."

"Then how do we prove it?"

Marian, with a mischievous look in her eyes and a smile tugging at her mouth, said, "I have an idea."

Chapter Sixty-One

"DID YOU SEE the way Marian looked at me?" Louise asked in a panicked tone as she wrung her hands.

"I did," Grant acknowledged. "Do you think she suspects something?"

Louise nodded. "I do. The thing that wretched Weaver woman said about flour turning her cat's fur gray raised Marian's antennae."

Grant began pacing around the spacious room. "But we were so careful. We never broke character, not even when we were by ourselves."

"If she tells the sheriff about her hunch when we can't get out of here, we're toast," Louise said miserably. "This was supposed to be easy, but that blasted ice storm messed everything up. If it hadn't been for that little twist of fate, we'd have hit our mark and been gone before anyone noticed."

Grant stopped his pacing and watched as his wife piled things into their suitcase. "What do you think you're doing?"

She dropped one of the matronly pairs of pants she'd packed into the suitcase, placed her hands on her hips, and turned to face him. "What does it look like I'm doing?" she snapped. "I'm packing. We have to get out of here."

"We can't leave. The roads are bad and I haven't retrieved the jewelry yet," he countered. "Besides, taking off unannounced will only make us look guilty. You saw the way they went after that Turner couple."

Louise sighed. "I suppose you're right. I'm telling you, though, the Bright woman suspects something. I saw the way her eyes narrowed. Something clicked in her brain about my hair."

Taking a few steps forward and grasping his wife's shoulders, Grant commanded, "Louise, you have to get hold of yourself. Nobody has any evidence. There hasn't even been any mention of the jewelry being found. Just let me retrieve it from that coat pocket I dropped it in, and we'll be golden. They've already searched our room, so there's no reason to do it again."

The woman's face twisted into a scowl. "That we know of."

"It will be okay. We're great at convincing people to believe what we want them to," Grant boasted. "I mean, look at you. You've played the role of self-doubting wife to a college professor beautifully! You couldn't be farther from that kind of woman, and that's why I love you."

Louise reluctantly nodded. "I suppose you're right. We'll stay here until the roads are clear enough to travel on, then promise me we can get out of here. I know how you like to push it to see how much you can get away with. Please don't do that this time."

Grant Hubley smiled. "I promise." He pulled his wife into

an embrace. "So, we're agreed; we'll stay here and act like everything is normal. We certainly make life interesting, don't we?"

She winked at her husband. "For better or worse."

"You make everything better. Especially our cons. You're a very brilliant lady." The admiration in his face reminded her why she'd ever agreed to such a harebrained idea as running cons for a living.

Louise had always dreamed of starring on Broadway, but these acting gigs paid much better.

Chapter Sixty-Two

AT MARIAN'S SUGGESTION, Joe and Eli had gathered all the Saddle Hill residents and were filling them in on Marian's theory and her plan to prove that the Hubleys were guilty, as well as the fact that Holly had seen Grant Hubley in the kitchen with a golden opportunity to drop the jewelry into her coat pocket.

"I remember seeing him in the kitchen, too, now that you mention it," Sylvia affirmed. "I didn't think anything of it at the time, and truthfully, I was too wrapped up in my own problems to pay any attention to him, but he was definitely in there."

Vito, who was standing near Sylvia, shot her a questioning look.

"We'll talk later," she said softly, then turned her attention back to the sheriff and his deputy.

Nodding in agreement, Vito did the same.

Joe looked out the window at the fading daylight. "At the request of Judge Becker, Eli and I will be taking shifts sitting up and keeping an eye on things. He made it perfectly clear that he doesn't want me calling him again."

"I think it would be a good idea to have one or two others here at all times as well," Marian interjected. "We'll take shifts so everybody at least gets a little sleep."

"That sounds like a good plan. Everybody, work out among yourselves who will be on watch and when. I'm taking the first shift, then Eli will take over around midnight," Joe announced to them. "Until your shifts, though, I would suggest that everyone head over to either Marian's or Vito's and get some rest. It's been quite a day."

Several folks murmured their agreement.

"We'll help clean up the kitchen," Sylvia volunteered, then she and Holly followed Ivy back to the kitchen.

The rest of them grabbed their coats and scarves, slipped them on, then went out into the frigid night.

"At least the ice stopped coming down," Patricia said to her husband.

"It's still slippery, though," James pointed out. "Be careful."

She nodded, her breath making small clouds in front of her face. "It will be for a while."

They looked up at the clear night sky, a million tiny stars winking at them from above. "It's such a beautiful night," James observed. "I wish we were home to enjoy it."

With round eyes, Patricia snapped her head around to look at James. "What kind of attitude is that, Santa Claus? Can't you enjoy a beautiful night anywhere? At least we're together." She tucked her hand in the crook of James's elbow and sighed. "How many Christmases have we been together?"

"Forty-two. It seems like all of them and not nearly enough

of them, all at the same time," James said, looking affectionately at his bride.

"I hope one day Kris gets as lucky as we have been." Patricia's tone was whimsical as she spoke.

A jolly laugh came somewhere from deep inside James. "It's not luck, Patty. It's hard work. At least, you've had to work hard to be patient with me and my Christmas shenanigans."

"That's true," the former Mrs. Claus agreed. "Still, I hope Kris is able to find happiness the way we have."

"He will, and if I'm not mistaken, he's already got his eye on the pretty little thing that works for Marian."

Chapter Sixty-Three

JOE SETTLED INTO the sofa in the sitting room for his shift of keeping an eye on the place—particularly the Hubleys. From his vantage point, he could see the hall that held the guest rooms and would be able to tell if anybody got up and tried to go to the kitchen during the night, but no one would be able to see him.

Assuming he could stay awake, that is.

He yawned as though punctuating his thought.

Sitting in a dark room in the middle of the night wasn't a recipe for staying awake, especially after sleeping poorly the night before.

He was sure the thief would try to retrieve the jewelry from Holly's coat pocket.

Joe smiled. Boy, was he in for a big surprise.

Chapter Sixty-Four

THE FARMHOUSE WAS dark and lonely. Despite the work Vito had done to restore the place, it was still a century old and had creaks that would never be fixed.

Ralph, taking the first shift, sat in the chair in Marian's office with a perfect view to the kitchen. If anybody tried to go in there, he'd see them.

He thought back to the Christmas before last, when his jewelry store had been robbed. Stockton's Jewel Palace was the only jewelry store in town, and his attention to detail, care for the customers, and fair prices ensured that it remained the only one. Never one to have enemies, he'd been hurt and flabbergasted that anyone would target him and his store.

As it turned out, his wife had been robbing him for months and stole a tennis bracelet worth several thousand dollars, not to mention the cash from the safe he kept at the store. The star had been stolen by Kris's brother, Nicholas, and planted in Kris's employee locker with the sole intention of framing Kris for the crime.

Unlike with Brenda, his wife at the time, a vendetta against Ralph had nothing to do with it.

Then there was Carla. Sweet, sweet Carla. She'd cracked his safe and taken the other star because she believed it was the best of Ralph in one single piece. He couldn't bring himself to press charges, and, after a quick annulment from Brenda, they were married only a few months later.

Things had changed so much since then, and yet here he was, helping set a trap for Saddle Hill's newest jewel thief. Based on the description of the diamond collar that had been stolen, it was probably worth twice as much as the bracelet Brenda had stolen from him.

Ralph sighed.

For so many years, there had been no crime in Saddle Hill. Now it seemed as though something happened every year—especially at Christmas.

He shook his head sadly. The world was changing, and Saddle Hill was changing right along with it.

Leaning back in the chair, Ralph laced his fingers behind his head, then crossed his legs at the ankles in what Carla said was his deep-in-thought position.

The sheriff was pretty sure he knew who the thief was, so as long as he made his move tonight, they'd catch him. On the other hand, it was supposed to be warmer and sunny tomorrow, giving the ice a chance to melt. If it did, and the thief was able to get away, they'd probably never find them.

This plan had to work, and it had to work tonight.

Chapter Sixty-Five

ELI TOSSED AND turned, his eyes refusing to stay closed. He still had a couple hours before he was due to take over for Joe, but he was restless.

As quietly as he could so as not to disturb the others in Vito's duplex, he swung his legs over the side of the sofa and crept toward the door. He slipped on his boots, laced them up, then opened the door. As he walked across the field to the refurbished farmhouse, he looked up at the sky. It was clear and black, with countless stars shining cheerfully above him.

Holly loved the stars and would have enjoyed seeing this.

Picking up his pace, Eli finally made it to the back door of the farmhouse and opened the door into the kitchen. He was greeted by Ralph, springing into action to catch the thief.

"What are you doing here?" Ralph asked, then glanced at his watch. "You still have two more hours."

"I couldn't sleep, and I thought my time would be better used here helping to keep an eye on things than laying on Vito's couch, frustrated that I couldn't fall asleep."

Ralph nodded in understanding, then pointed in the direction of the sitting room. "Joe's in there, probably half asleep by now."

Eli smiled slightly, thanked Ralph, and went off to find his partner.

As Ralph had predicted, Joe sat in a chair tucked away in the corner, his eyes heavy and struggling to stay open.

"You look like you could use some shuteye," Eli observed.

Joe's head snapped up and he rubbed his eyes. "What are you doing here?"

"Ralph asked me the same thing. I'm starting to feel unwelcome," Eli teased.

"Sorry." Joe cleared his throat. "I've got the first shift."

A smirk twisting his mouth, Eli waved a hand in his direction. "Clearly."

Straightening in his chair, Joe asked, "What are you really doing here?"

Eli shrugged and settled onto the sofa. "I couldn't sleep, so I figured I might as well come help. Or, considering how exhausted you seem to be, go ahead and take over."

"I could use some sleep," Joe admitted. "I really don't want to go back over to the barn, though."

Eli thought for a minute. "Why don't you go sleep in Josephine's room? She's with Nadine at Marian's house, so she won't be needing it tonight."

Using an index finger, Joe tapped on the side of his head. "This is why I keep you around."

The deputy's mouth drooped. "To find places for you to sleep? Glad I can help," he remarked, dryly.

Joe rose from his chair and pointed to it. "Sit here. That

way you can see anybody coming down the hall, but they can't see you." He turned to walk down the hall and toward the stairs that led to the second floor. "I'll have my phone on in case you need me." Then he was gone, in search of rest.

Eli settled into the chair that Joe had directed him to sit, crossed his ankle over his knee, and took a deep breath. By tomorrow morning this could all be over. The thief might have been apprehended, the warmer temperatures and sunshine might have melted the ice enough for them to return to normal life. He appreciated Marian and Vito's hospitality of feeding them and letting them all crash at their home, but he wanted time with just Holly. They were still newlyweds, after all.

Besides, he had something important he wanted to tell her.

Chapter Sixty-Six

THE NUMBERS ON the bedside clock glowed green. It was one o'clock in the morning, and Grant Hubley had yet to close his eyes.

"You awake?" he whispered.

"Yeah, who could sleep?" his wife replied.

"When do you think I should make my move?" He stared at the bedroom ceiling, his eyes fully adjusted to the darkness.

Louise rolled onto her side, then pushed up onto her elbow facing him. "I don't know. I'm sure everyone is asleep by now. It's been dark for hours. Other than us, the Turners, and that Weaver woman, no one else is sleeping in the farmhouse. I suppose now is as good a time as any."

Grant tightened his lips into a thin line. "Did you mean what you said before? About wanting a different kind of life? Or were you still in character?"

Louise sighed and dropped back down onto her pillow. "Yes, I suppose I did mean it. When I went into acting, it was to bring joy to people and try to help them forget about their problems. Or at least help them identify with the character I was playing. Now I don't bring joy to people. I bring sadness and insurance claims."

"You know I'd do anything to make you happy. If you're discontent with this life now, this will be our last job," Grant promised. "We have to see this one through, though. We've already been paid, and the client is counting on us to deliver."

With a smile and a nod of her head, Louise wrapped her arms around her husband's neck. "Thank you."

"Anything for you, babe." He glanced again at the clock. "I might as well get this over with," he said as he sat up and climbed out of bed. Throwing his regular clothes back on, he then tied his shoes and turned back to her. "Wish me luck."

"Good luck," Louise whispered back.

∽

Eli perked up at the faint sound of hinges creaking. Grabbing his phone, he shot a quick text to Joe to let him know somebody was moving around.

Holding his breath so he didn't give away his presence, Eli slowly rose from his chair and took one sideways step deeper into the shadows.

As he squinted in the darkness, the unmistakable creak of a floorboard put him into high alert.

Soft footsteps padded past him, and he wondered if Ralph was still watching the kitchen or if he'd been relieved by someone else. Whoever it was, Eli hoped they were able-bodied in case there was a scuffle.

Following the path of the footsteps, he walked slowly and silently through the house until he reached the kitchen.

He placed a hand on the wall, groping for the light switch. When he found it, he flipped it on, illuminating the kitchen in bright light.

A man stood with his back to Eli, his hand inside Holly's coat pocket. He cursed then whipped around to face the deputy.

"What kind of game is this?" Grant Hubley growled.

Eli glanced at the man's hand and saw that he was holding the chain Marian had taken off her tea strainer as a decoy and placed in the pocket that had once held Onyx's diamond collar. He grinned. It was a good switch. "It's the kind of game where you lose."

Vito stood in the doorway of Marian's office, Sylvia beside him. "You know, it's not nice to steal a lady's jewelry," Vito scolded.

Grant Hubley narrowed his eyes at the small group. "You knew? But *how*?"

"I didn't actually have any idea, until somebody mentioned that your wife smelled very strongly of baby powder. I remembered seeing a big bottle of baby powder in your bathroom when we were doing the search, but still didn't connect the dots. Cassandra Weaver tipped Marian off when she mentioned how her cat got into flour one time and turned herself gray," Eli explained.

With a scowl on his face, Grant rolled his eyes. "Stupid."

"Oh, it was a good plan, but you had to have known you couldn't keep it up forever."

Grant shrugged. "We didn't have to keep it up forever. We decided this was our last job."

"Job?" Eli clarified. "You mean you were hired for this?"

Clamping his lips shut, Grant Hubley crossed his arms over his chest, signaling that he wouldn't be doing any more talking.

The theft was solved, and the mystery now was finding out who hired the Hubleys to steal the jewelry in the first place.

Chapter Sixty-Seven

WHEN MORNING DAWNED, the sun was shining brilliantly and the temperature outside was warmer than it had been the two days prior. Icicles fell off the edges of the roof, shattering as they hit the ground and bringing with them the hope that everyone would soon be able to get back to their normal lives.

The aroma of fresh coffee filled the air and something baking in the oven added to the mouthwatering scent.

Judge Becker, grumpy at having been bothered once again, signed arrest warrants for Grant and Louise Hubley. Eli, with his service weapon, and Vito with a rolling pin he'd swiped from the kitchen, stood guard outside the door of their suite while Joe took care of the details of transporting them to jail. When he hung up the phone, he joined his deputy and Vito and filled them in.

"As suspected, our criminals aren't really named Grant and Louise Hubley. Their real names are Rob and Doris Hodges. They're thieves for hire any time someone wants something bad enough to pay through the nose for it. Evidently, their services don't come cheap."

Eli furrowed his brow. "But who hired them?"

"According to our prisoners," Joe said with a quick tilt of his head toward the door to the Hubleys'/Hodges' suite, "Cassandra Weaver's abusive ex-husband hired them."

Vito's eyes widened and his mouth fell open. "I thought he didn't know where she was."

Joe sighed. "She thinks he doesn't. He's been keeping tabs on her since she left him, though, and recently realized she'd taken a valuable piece of heirloom jewelry with her when she left. It had been her grandmother's, but he decided he wanted it even though he had no right to it."

"That's disgusting," Eli growled.

"It sure is. Turns out Cassandra's grandmother went to a lot of political parties and wore a diamond choker to most of them. It was her signature piece. When Cassandra rescued Onyx from the shelter, she had the choker made into a collar for her cat. Some people just have more money than sense," Joe muttered, shaking his head.

Vito nodded slightly, but said, "I get it, though. If that cat was loyal and loving to her when her husband was abusing her, it's only natural that she would hold it in high regard."

"I guess so…" Joe reluctantly agreed. "On a very, very good note, the ice is melting and the road crews are out. We should be able to get out of here in the next couple of hours. I'll take over from here, Vito."

With the rolling pin in his hand and his shoulders sagging, Vito came to the realization that he didn't want Sylvia to go anywhere. He liked having her around, and the prospect of her going back to her regular life without him didn't sit well.

It's now or never, he told himself, then straightened his shoulders and went to find the big-city fashion designer who had told him fashion was overrated.

Chapter Sixty-Eight

AS THE SADDLE Hill residents gathered their things to head back to their own homes, Sylvia carefully folded the clothes Vito had let her borrow and held them for a few moments before walking back to the farmhouse where Marian, Vito, Joe, and Eli were. Dressed in the clothes she came in, she crossed the field between the house and the converted barn. Walking through the back door and into the kitchen, she was greeted by Vito, who was wearing a frown.

"Just the man I was looking for," Sylvia said as she extended the neatly folded pile of clothes toward him. "Thanks for letting me borrow these."

He took the clothes from her and mumbled, "Anytime."

"Now that the ice is melting, I guess we'll be out of your hair and you can go back to business as usual," she said, trying to sound cheerful but knowing the attempt fell flat.

"Guess so."

Sylvia chewed her bottom lip and glanced around the kitchen. For the first time since they got iced in, it wasn't bustling with activity. "You know," she finally said, "I'm going to be in Saddle Hill another couple of weeks. Would you want to do something before I head back?"

Vito's head snapped up and he looked at her as if trying to determine if she was serious. Deciding she was, he said, "Yes. I would. Very much."

A megawatt smile lit up Sylvia's face and was mirrored on Vito's. She reached into her pocket and pulled out a slip of paper. "This is my cell number. Use it," she commanded playfully.

"Yes, ma'am," Vito agreed, the smile never leaving his eyes.

"I need to get going. Talk to you soon?"

Vito nodded. "Very soon."

Sylvia smiled as she walked away. It was time to find balance in her life and give some attention to her personal life.

This Christmas was going to turn out perfect, after all.

Chapter Sixty-Nine

MARIAN WATCHED AS two of her guests were loaded into the sheriff's car. She shook her head sadly.

"I guess you just never know about some people," a voice said from behind her.

Turning around, Marian came eye to eye with Cassandra Weaver.

"I'm so sorry this happened to you," Marian said.

A sigh from the other woman preceded her words. "It's not your fault. Tom—that's my ex—promised he'd find a way to keep tabs on me and to make me pay for walking out on him. He shouted that threat at my back, but I kept going. I'm honestly surprised I lived to tell about it. I never would have thought he'd try to steal my grandmother's diamonds, though."

In a wave of compassion, Marian reached out and placed her hand on the woman's shoulder. "You are more than welcome to stay here as long as you need to. You *and* Onyx. On the house, of course. No one should be alone at Christmas."

Footsteps interrupted the moment.

"We're going to head out," Wes Turner informed Marian. "Sorry for causing such a mess around here."

Marian smiled at the burly man with the permanent scowl. "No apology necessary." She looked back and forth between Cassandra and Wes. "I'm hosting Christmas here. If you don't have anywhere else to go, I would love it if you could be here."

Tears sprang into Cassandra's eyes, and Wes looked touched as well.

"Chrissy and I will talk about it," the man promised. "Thanks for everything." He walked out of the kitchen, leaving Marian to hope he and his wife would seriously consider her invitation.

"I'll think about it, too," Cassandra vowed, then turned and walked in the direction of her suite.

Raising her eyes to the ceiling, Marian had a deep sense of well-being. Though the ice had left the guests panicked, the time spent together brought transformation for them all.

"Roger, you would have loved this," Marian whispered to her deceased husband, then set about the task of giving the kitchen a deep clean.

Christmas would be here before they knew it, and she had to be ready.

Epilogue

Christmas Day

A LIGHT SNOW FELL on Saddle Hill. It was a white Christmas even though the local meteorologist said there was no chance of having one. Obviously, he didn't know the kind of magic Christmas brought to the town.

The Christmas tree in the corner winked its lights as though it knew the secrets of everyone there. The scent of fresh pine filled the room while the votive candles, carefully nestled in the greenery running the length of the table, flickered happily. Even the pine cones tucked in beside them conveyed a message of stability.

For the ones there to witness it, it truly was the most wonderful time of the year.

Several Saddle Hill residents and a few newcomers gathered around the table at the Farmhouse Inn Bed & Breakfast. Faces were aglow with the joy of the season, each one thankful for another year together.

Cassandra Weaver had taken Marian up on her offer and had been living at the bed-and-breakfast the last couple weeks. Despite the fact that Marian had offered her suite to her free of charge, Cassandra was determined to work off her debt to the woman. As it turned out, she was a phenomenal cook and Marian often put her in charge of baking treats to place in the guests' rooms at check-in. Marian saw potential in the woman and wondered if perhaps Ms. Weaver would be her next hire.

Wes and Chrissy Turner showed up minutes before dinner was served, surprising everyone there except Marian. She'd had a hunch they'd come. They explained that being on the move all the time didn't feel like the freedom Wes was searching for. Instead, for the first time since Wes got out of jail, they felt freedom to be themselves in the company of this group of people. The husband and wife also announced that they were looking for a fresh start and were considering making Saddle Hill their home. Permanently.

Sylvia and Vito sat shoulder-to-shoulder, fingers intertwined under the table. Their first date had quickly become a second and third, then Sylvia gave Vito the best Christmas gift of all. After many long and detailed discussions with her second-in-command, she turned over the day-to-day operations of Jersey Belle, but the two agreed that she would retain creative control. She would now spend half her time in New York, and the other half at her home in Saddle Hill. With that decision made, Sylvia felt as though a huge weight had been lifted from her shoulders. She was on a quest for balance, and for the first time in her adult life, felt like it was within reach.

Vito couldn't believe his good fortune that the most beautiful woman he'd ever laid eyes on was considering a future with him. What he'd come to realize over the past couple of weeks was that Sylvia was even more beautiful on the inside. Ever since he first met her last Christmas when she came to the farmhouse looking for Marian, she'd been on his mind. Despite their differences, they had enough in common to make things work, and he couldn't wait to see what the future held.

When they were able to go home and have some time alone, Eli told Holly that he was ready to start having kids. Though she was taken aback, Holly thought of how much fun she had with Josephine and quickly got used to the idea of having their own. The decision came not a moment too soon, because Holly realized they already had a little one on the way the day after the roads were clear enough for them to leave the bed-and-breakfast.

Ralph was thrilled to have Sylvia spend more time in Saddle Hill. Their business relationship had turned into a solid friend-ship, and he felt as though she belonged in Kentucky. He was also overjoyed that he'd be able to retain his position as jewelry designer for Jersey Belle. The lucrative position had meant that he didn't have to worry about making enough sales to keep Stockton's Jewel Palace open. The store, which had become more of a well-loved hobby than a means of income, would continue to serve as a creative outlet for him as long as he wanted to keep going.

Joe and Nadine sat in contented silence as the baby moni-tor they'd placed on the table in front of them showed Josephine asleep with a smile on her face. This would be their only Christmas as a trio, and Nadine vowed to relish every moment of it. She still hadn't told Joe their family would be growing; that was something better saved until they were home by them-selves later tonight. It would be tough to balance a toddler, a new baby, and a job, but with Marian as her boss, Nadine was confident that she'd have plenty of help.

With smiles punctuating the joy of the season, James and

Patricia Jingle sat with their oldest son, again thankful that their friends were more like family. Patricia was writing another book, entitled *Life After Mrs. Claus*, a memoir about her adjustment to a normal life after forty years of playing the role day in and day out. James, on the other hand, continued to play Santa at the mall between Thanksgiving and Christmas, happily listening to the children as they gave him their wish lists. Patricia often said, "You can take the man out of Christmas, but you can't take Christmas out of the man."

Kris had just gotten his first job teaching English literature at the local high school. Though it was a part-time gig and his goal was to teach at the college level, he viewed the opportunity as a springboard into bigger things. Deciding to take another leap, he had asked Ivy out on a date and she'd readily agreed. Optimistic about where their relationship might go, he had none of the doubts he'd had when he was going out with Carol Ling last year.

Marian, lovingly scanning each of the faces at the table, was overcome with joy that she had people to share this day with. Since losing Roger, the ones who were now gathered at her table made her feel less alone. They welcomed her just as she welcomed them. As tears sprang to her eyes, she smiled at the good fortune that always seemed to find her at Christmastime. With the crew that surrounded her now, she was certain it would be this way for years to come.

Dear Reader,

Thank you so much for spending time in Saddle Hill. I hope you've enjoyed it there as much as I have. I have come to love the characters and wish they were real people. Marian, especially, would be so much fun to know, and I'd love to try one of Nadine's Christmas cookies.

Though the series has come to an end, I'm thinking of ways to visit Saddle Hill again – though maybe not at Christmas.

I appreciate the time you've invested in these characters and this town, and I hope you'll find enjoyment in my other books as well.

All the best,

Erin

Acknowledgements

As always, no writer is an island. It takes many capable hands to take the book from an idea to something worth putting in the hands of you, the reader. Many thanks are in order for the creation of this book, and I can never adequately express my gratitude to those who have worked with me.

To editor extraordinaire, Dierdre Stoelzle, who consistently provides a keen eye for detail and is generous with her encouraging comments while at the same time suggesting ways to make the story better.

To the wonderful folks at Damonza, for creating a beautiful book, inside and out.

To my husband, Billy, and daughters, Zoe and Nora, as well as many friends and family who have encouraged me through this process. You have no idea how much your support means to me!

Thank you to Barbara Napier, whose bed and breakfast was the inspiration for the Farmhouse Inn Bed & Breakfast in this book. I hope my fictional characters felt as welcome there as I always have at Snug Hollow.

Finally, to you, the reader. Without you, there would be no reason to write! Thank you for taking a chance on the Saddle Hill series. I hope it has provided you with many hours of good entertainment and that you have enjoyed reading this story as much as I enjoyed writing it.

www.ingramcontent.com/pod-product-compliance
Lightning Source LLC
Chambersburg PA
CBHW061806190726
48289CB00007B/2091